SINGLES

Elizabeth O'Hara

D1609756

ABOUT THE AUTHOR

Elizabeth O'Hara is the pseudonym of a major new author for Basement Press. Her fiction has previously been published by Irish, English and American presses.

Basement Press
DUBLIN

First published in Ireland in 1994 by
Basement Press
4 Upper Mount Street
Dublin 2

A catalogue record for this title is available from the British Library

ISBN 1 855940 574

Singles is a work of fiction. Any resemblance to real characters, organisations or events is purely coincidental.

The moral right of Elizabeth O'Hara to be identified as the author of this work is asserted.

Cover Design: Eva Burns
Origination: Verbatim Typesetting and Design
Printing: The Guernsey Press Co Ltd.

This book is published with the assistance of The Arts Council/An Chomhairle Ealaíon.

DEDICATION

For Síle

CHAPTER ONE

The train snores along a narrow track. Feathery
bushels of steam issue from its brass chimney.
The engine man shovels coal into the furnace;
the guard blows a silver whistle. Past fields of
corn, low green hills and meandering streams
the engine pulls a string of toytown carriages.

Nuala is standing in an accordion-pleated
corridor. A young man with black hair encircles
her in his arm and kisses her. The corridor
sways dramatically. Nuala has seldom felt so
happy.

They approach a little town, a tussock of
spires and russet roofs dozing among the hills.

Nuala slips from the man's embrace to look
out the window. She stares at a duck-pond.

The guard blows his whistle again.

And when Nuala turns around, the dark
haired man, her man, has disappeared.

She knows he has stepped off the train into
the fields, into the duck-pond, maybe, though
the train has not stopped or even slowed down.
She knows he has gone.

What she feels is a fragile sense of surprise.

'Nuala, Nuala, wake up! You'll be late!'

1

Nuala stirred under her pile of blankets, opened her eyes. In the doorway her mother was framed—night-tossed hair, morning grey complexion. Man's tartan dressing-gown fastened with a tie.

'Get up, alannah! It's eight o'clock. You don't want to be late the first day, do you?'

'It's OK, I'm coming.'

The train slips along its coal-black track. Nuala wished she could stay aboard, wished she could sleep for longer just to find out where the train is going and how the dream is going to end.

'Dreams don't end, that's the trouble with dreams!' Reluctantly she stuck her legs out on to the flowery fawn carpet and forced the rest of her body after them. The air in the room was freezing, even though it was only mid-October. 'They're turned off, that's what happens to them. Always long before they're finished.'

She pulled on the pink dressing-gown she got from Santy when she was eleven and plodded across the landing to the bathroom, which was not a real bathroom but a partitioned section of the landing, one of the many partitions and extensions, additions and improvements, in this dark and uncomfortable house. (Nuala's father is a compulsive do-it-yourselfer. As well as this bathroom, which contains a toilet, tiny washbasin, and shower which has never functioned from the first day it

2

was installed, there is a large bathroom down at the back of the kitchen and an open-air toilet perched in the middle of a large wooden shed around at the side door. Nuala has not used that for years, and supposes that nobody else has either. Who uses a free range-toilet?

She regarded her face in the mirror. As anyone would, washing in front of it in the early morning. As she would have done in a tent in darkest Africa, in an igloo at the North Pole, on board a paper bark crossing the Atlantic. Looking, peering, hunting. For what? For beauty of course, what does any girl aged twenty-two look for?

And saw? A bony white face, eyes a pale grey, nose too long, mouth narrow, eyebrows heavy. Hair red and tousled like leaves on a windy tree. Skin translucent. Because Nuala was thin, half-starved. You could nearly see through her.

Beauty. It depends. That is the problem. Sometimes the mirror says yes and sometimes no.

She smiled, wiped her face with a hard facecloth and admired the red flush which arose in response to the icy water. Yes, the answer seemed to be, today. For the time being.

She returned to the bedroom and took from the wardrobe a selection of clothes carefully assembled the night before: blue bell-bottom jeans, a blue and white checked blouse, a navy cardigan. Striped navy socks and black platform shoes completed her idea of an appropriate outfit for a working girl. (Girl is the word, her own and everybody else's, for a female of twenty-two. Nuala did not know that when she reached forty-two some people would still apply this word to her, nor did she care.) Quickly, to defeat the morning chill, she pulled everything on, covering every inch of her semi-transparent body.

She did not know it was semi-transparent. She knew that through it could be seen her bones and veins, but not that you could also see her thoughts and feelings. Her plans and ambitions and her terrible fears.

But you could. In two seconds flat you could know everything that she thought is a secret closely guarded by her denim clothes and pale skin and shy diffident voice. Just as you could see right behind her Mary, her older sister, sleeping in the second bed in this high cold room.

Mary, Mary, quite beautiful, rosy with sleep. Her hair black as Snow White's. Her skin thick as parchment. Her eyes clamped shut. Mary you could not see through at all. She was herself, her own secret. She smiled in her sleep and turned smoothly in the bed like a mermaid flipping through a friendly wave. She emitted a silvery whistle. What is Mary dreaming of? What is Mary thinking? Only Mary knew.

Certainly Nuala hadn't the foggiest.

Running downstairs to breakfast.

Running down the road to the bus-stop. Running down the street to the office.

Her first day at her first job after graduation. Oh yes! A big day. An exciting day. Independence, a new career, a new road opening wide before her. What she felt, for the first time in her whole life, was despair.

Surely this was not the way it should be?

'Ah sure it's just nerves.' She used her mother's voice to console herself as she approached the eggbox which housed her new office. 'Things are always better than you think they are. Don't be worrying yourself.'

Nuala's mother really did not know why Nuala was taking this job, a job in the Civil Service which she could have had four years ago, before she had her BA in English and her first class MA and her long dull thesis on Middle English homiletic prose behind her. What was all the studying and the midnight oil for? Her mother had given up trying to understand Nuala long ago, about the time she had refused to do French or Irish or Geography, and had insisted on the superior merits of Old and Middle English. Her mother, like a lot of other people, did not know what Old English was, let alone Middle. And how an expert knowledge of the gobbledegook from which poems called *Beowulf* or 'Wulf and Eadwacker' came qualified people for jobs in the Civil Service which in the recent past had been filled by people with three honours in the Leaving was even harder to understand. Nuala's mother had given up.

'Maybe it'll be fun,' the interior Mammy said cheerfully. The interior Mammy must never give up. 'Maybe it'll be just wonderful. And anyway,' trudging up the wide flagged steps, 'it's only for a while. You will move on. Of course you will!'

Just what Robin Allgood, her teacher, tutor, supervisor—her hero, her god, her father substitute, her mother substitute—had said.

'Oh I shouldn't worry,' he'd stammered in his endearing way, staring over the rims of his spectacles. 'You'll probably get used to the change. And let's face it, nobody can expect to get work with Old English.'

Nobody except for people like him. Robin Allgood, the learned, the kindly, the stereotypical scholar, instantly recognisable as such to anyone who has ever read a satire on English university. (There are no satires on Irish universities but they are not necessary, the lecturers here are cut from much the same pattern as the David Lodge lot. Change the accents, slightly, but not the clothes or the attitudes.) In Robin's case you didn't have to change the accent either, since he was a native speaker. A native speaker of Sweet's Anglo-

6

Saxon, some said with friendly malice. Eccentric, absent-minded, head in some medieval cloud of unknowing. Surprisingly enough, he was the one and only teacher Nuala had met in her four years in college with whom she had had anything that could be termed a friendship. Boys sometimes became friendly with their lecturers and gained some sort of patronage or support. Girls could, in those pre-PC days, have affairs with the more flamboyant and trendy ones—of which there were two—or else be ignored. Nuala was ignored. Her skinny body and red hair, her irregular features and copious freckles, did not inspire men whose ideal of feminine beauty was a cross between Blanche of Gaunt and Marilyn Monroe. Her mind—well, who cared about her mind ? It was reported that the professor of English had once said at a party that women—in general—didn't have any. Not in the sense that men had. In his company, and in that of most of his staff, Nuala and the other girls certainly acted as if they were bordering on the moronic. The fact that—in general—they got higher marks than boys in examinations did not increase their self-confidence one bit. The consensus was that those results came about as some sort of fluke. Maybe the girls were cuter in the management of time. Maybe they were goody-goodies. Swots. Nothing in their behaviour or conversation outside the examination halls suggested

7

that they were intelligent. Their minds were sometimes quick and sometimes their insights were original and penetrating. But they lacked the intellectual sturdiness or stamina that characterised the best boys. There was something flimsy about them. Maybe that explained why all the best girl graduates ended up as housewives, schoolteachers and librarians while the best boy graduates became university professors, ambassadors or managing directors. The girls did better in examinations but not in life. With them it was all a flash in the youthful pan.

The only person who had ever encouraged Nuala was Robin. Dear old odd Robin. The one lecturer she had ever truly admired. A truly perceptive man, a true scholar. He read *Beowulf* on the number ten bus. Proof of exceptional dedication and intellect. And then there was his style. Conversational style, that is, because as far as dress was concerned he was always rigged out in the regulation tweed jacket and corduroy trousers. But he spoke with Ciceronian panache. No metaphor was too risky, no rhetorical flourish too outlandish. He even went as far as to speak Latin—on rare occasions, it is true. "Nulle dies since lineis," he would roar when some student had forgotten to do their translation. And then he would translate for the benefit of those who had not had a classical education: 'No day without its lions'.

And he insisted on regarding Fairfield University as a real institution of learning, not a factory for the production of teachers. He appeared to respect the students and assume that they shared his own attitude, rather than taking it for granted that—in general—they were silly nuisances. Robin used words such as scholarship to second year undergraduates. 'This is not scholarship,' he had said to Nuala, handing her back an essay on *Njal's Saga*. (He threw in some Old Norse, on the side, just in case Old English was not old and odd enough for you.) 'You must learn to write a scholarly paper!' The thrill of it, to one who thought of scholarship as a term designating a certain, usually meagre, sum of money dispensed by Dublin Corporation in a manila envelope to the poor but bright. The delight of hearing the fine old Anglo-Saxon word. Her heart, tightly stuffed with the traditional Irish sentimental love of learning as well as what she suspected was a true love of learning, had warmed to him then, even though he'd given her a 'C'. C from a man like that was worth an A from one who said 'research'.

She'd been sure he'd be the one to pull her back into the fold, to encourage her to stay on a do a PhD, to offer her hope. Instead he'd said, 'You'll get used to it, I dare say!' and then, 'Excuse me, there's the phone.'

And here she was, like some virgin martyr,
stepping into the Department of the European
Environment, taking up her job as a civil
servant, the job which undergraduates in
English scoffed at almost as much as they
scoffed at secondary school teaching—a job
which Nuala secretly suspected she would
enjoy, but which her friends, who had vague
and crude notions about what was then called
women's lib, had derided so much as a typical
women's job that she had not dared even to
consider it.

It was not that she had no alternative.
Indeed, she had already learned that life always
offered alternatives at times when it might have
been much simpler to do without them. Always
two parties, two boyfriends, and now two jobs.
Choices, crossroads, decisions. And nobody to
help you make them. How could her mother,
who had left school at the age of fourteen, as
she never tired of repeating, help Nuala, who
had left it at the age of twenty-two and seemed
sometimes to know everything? Nuala's father
had never been one to offer advice to anyone,
least of all to his daughters, of whom he was
frightened. They seemed to belong not just to a
different sex but to a different species from him.

That's how she thought of it later. But in fact
Nuala had had advisers just as she had had
choices. It was just that at the time she didn't
take the advice and it hadn't felt like much of a

choice. Still, the truth was that when she had made her decision to work in the Civil Service, at least one other way of life had been immediately open to her. In Ireland in the 1970s everyone talked incessantly about unemployment and the job problem but in reality anyone with any reasonable qualifications had a range of options. There was some unwritten rule, however, which said that nobody was allowed to admit this. Maybe the society was unable to believe its good luck—and it did turn out to be short-lived. The summer Nuala got her BA, she'd been surprised at the number of jobs she was offered. It seemed all you had to do was apply, and you got them! All those offers she'd turned down because she couldn't bear to stop studying. The summer she got her MA, this summer, the offers were not so plentiful. Maybe she was getting too old. And the MA put people off.

Even so, as well as the Civil Service job she had got a much more congenial post as a lecturer in English as a Foreign Language— which is obviously quite different from real English—at an Algerian university, the University of Oran. Two testy brown men in safari shirts had interviewed her for this post in a bedroom in the Burlington Hotel. They had expressed wonder that she would want such a position but had made the offer nonetheless. And they had been kind, putting her in touch with a woman who had held the job during the previous year. Nuala went to visit her. She lived in a huge dilapidated house on Sorrento Terrace, with a baby and a red setter and a neat handsome husband who looked as if he rode horses. The woman, whose name was Lucy Ann—she *was* a Lucy Ann—had driven to Oran in a Morris Minor (of course!) with the baby in a carrycot on the back seat. Her husband had gone over for the holidays, she said, smiling in the wistful pre-Raphaelite way which characterised her. She glanced at him alluringly as she proferred this piece of information, so that Nuala, not quite interpreting what the glance meant, sensed enough to feel envious. This relationship seemed so perfect. The house was marvellous, a kind of house only faintly familiar to Nuala but utterly desirable: old, full of antique bric-à-brac, bygones of one kind and another, with red handwoven carpets hanging on the walls. They'd bought these in Algeria and hoped to sell them. Would Nuala know of anyone? This detracted from the romance, but only marginally. She demurred and continued to gaze in awe at this perfect couple.

She was willowy, in a long flimsy gown of some kind, possibly muslin, possibly an antique tea-gown. Her features were delicate and babyish; she had wide grey eyes and wispy shiny curling brown hair. And he was stocky and small and virile. They seemed so deeply in love, seemed so unable to conceal this even for a moment, as they stood and chatted to Nuala, glowing in their own joy, that she felt obliged to let them know that she had a boyfriend, that he was away at present but soon would return, that he would certainly want to visit her in Algeria and did they think that would be permissible—some things they had told her had suggested that it was a police state.

They did think so, oh yes they certainly did, and then they offered Nuala a cup of coffee in their huge pine kitchen. And as they stood at the breakfast counter and drank, or as Nuala and the husband drank, because the woman of course refused, she was the type of woman who looked as if she hardly ever drank or ate anything, the type of woman who really does look like some kind of supernatural being, a nymph or a water sprite or something, they talked about Oran. How wonderful it was, one of the most wonderful cities in the world. The view as you approached it was one of the finest imaginable. It was said to be more lovely than the view of Venice from the harbour. And it was socialist, which was interesting, and a lot of people spoke French, which is always nice. And the poverty was appalling. It was like an overheated Moscow. She would live in a high-rise apartment block and have just about enough money to survive, and there would be an awful lot of awfully basic teaching, and she'd spend an awful lot of time making photocopies on an old and inadequate Gestetner machine. Nuala wondered what it was she would be copying. She had seldom photocopied anything. There was a new Xerox machine in the students' union in Fairfield, but it cost twopence a page to make a copy and there was always a long queue. She had found it more convenient to transcribe any information she needed directly from the books she read in the library. Although the thought of having to deal with something as technical as a copying machine worried her, she was generally enthralled by Lucy Ann's account of Algerian life. A great wanderlust filled her, a yearning to travel across Europe down to the south, all the way to the Mediterannean, which she had never seen, all the way to Africa. She could see Oran glittering in shades of dark-gold, shimmering bronze, hugged by a wine-red sea. Standing in Lucy Ann's breakfast nook, she knew she had to go. Out there she would escape from whatever it was the oppressed her at home. She would find the freedom that eluded her in Ireland, and she would become a new and vigorous and better person. There would be an end to the narrow lanes there in the great open deserts, the burning seas, the high-rise apartments. Away. Abroad.

'Oh yes, you must go,' Lucy Ann gently urged, letting her out into the gloom of Dalkey.

'And please write and let me know how it goes!'

Another person had urged her to take the job in Oran. No less a person than the careers and appointments officer in Fairfield, to Nuala's great surprise and to his eternal credit.

'Don't take the EO,' he said, swivelling in his director's chair towards his view of the square grey Fairfield lake. ' You'll be bored. The EO...' Words seemed to fail him. He looked at the pond, pondering. This new project of the Civil Service, funded by borrowed money and devised to employ the rush of graduates who were suddenly emerging from the universities in unprecedented numbers thanks to Donagh O'Malley and his scheming, was proving to be trickier than it had seemed initially. It was all very well to boast about offers of jobs and government concern to keep graduates at home, but as a careers officer you had to try to keep square pegs out of round holes if at all possible. The girls were the hardest to rescue. It seemed that some of them were absolutely addicted to square holes and could not even imagine finding a career that would suit them. 'You'll be bored, probably.' He smiled in an avuncular way at Nuala. She looked very small and young as she sat in a huge green cube of a chair. Had she nobody to look after her at all?

'You should go to Algeria,' he said. 'It will suit you better than the Civil Service.' And he went on to talk about duty to the Third World and how we all settled down sooner than we thought and didn't get these opportunities any more. Nuala half-listened. She was staring at his office. She'd never known rooms like this existed in Fairfield. All the rooms she'd ever used or visited were grey, hard and untidy. The students had hard grey corridors and narrow grey lockers. The lecturers had narrow grey rooms. The professors had slightly larger rooms, also grey, with plastic tiles on the floors and flourescent lights in the ceiling. You had to be in Administration, apparently, to get thick carpet, potted plants, picture windows framing a view of flowery shrubs, the lake and the odd Canada goose on day release from Stephen's Green.

'Think about it,' he finished up. He owed some loyalty to the Civil Service since he'd been involved in devising their latest ghastly scheme. Besides he was not supposed to make up any student's mind for him or her. 'But go,' he called, fired by an unprofessional instinct, as she pushed the door. 'Go!' He had a daughter himself with a talent for painting.

Nuala tramped downstairs and across the yard to the shabby new Arts Block with an air of great resolution and renewed faith in humanity. To think that the Careers and Appointments Officer, someone whom she had assumed to be on a par with parents or university lecturers as far as jobs were concerned, people who seemed to lack all imagination and ambition and to believe that the only requirement was money and security, that nothing else mattered, actually had the courage and wit to advise her not to grab this meal ticket but to set off on an adventure instead, to take her future and life and limb and transport them to the north of Africa, to the dark-gold wastes where the outsider had moaned and groaned...Hope! There was hope for everyone, even for her.

But a week later Nuala had written to the Civil Service Commission and accepted their offer of an appointment, and penned a short note of regret to the University of Oran. Why? Not because she was a masochist. Not because she was a coward, not because she had given one second's thought to a regular income or an old age pension. None of these factors had anything to do with her decision.

It was because of Erik.

The love factor.

A phenomenon not recognised by the readers of women's curricula vitae, by compilers of career statistics. The simple explanation of roads not travelled, offers rejected, successes scorned. What employer could take it into account, what feminist, examining the dismal figures, seriously consider it? A factor too silly, too old-fashioned, to be admitted by the most chauvinistic male manager. That girls under the age of twenty, or even thirty, in the mid 1970s, educated liberated girls with egalitarian expectations, counted fragile relationships with sometimes diffident men to be of greater moment than any number of academic qualifications or interesting careers. Married women, their emotional needs fulfilled, forget their youthful insecurity. It's easy to be ambitious and feminist when you've found you've taken care of your emotional and biological needs. Not so easy when everything you see and hear indicates that your first duty is to find a mate, and when your inner voice, the voice of your mother, perhaps, whispers all the time that you'll never really be happy without one. Moreover, that your mammy won't respect you unless you do. All that learning and all those books and all those essays you wrote were just a way of filling in time, maybe, or a sort of insurance policy in case you missed the boat you were really aiming to catch all along. Or a way, Nuala sometimes thought, observing a lot of her female friends, of deflecting attention from the true pursuit so that it would not seem as blatant and vulgar as it had been in the past, if Jane Austen's accounts, for instance, were anything to go by. A new version of hard-to-get. Falling in love with your subject was a hazard you were supposed to avoid. It was a game you played until you'd got your degree and your man. Nuala had committed an error of taste and judgment in getting attached to work. Even Robin Allgood seemed to think so. A passion for learning or for literature was as inappropriate in a young woman as any other kind of passion, it seemed. The thing to be was cool.

In the event, Nuala was. When it came to the crunch she had no difficulty in betraying her love for English or her ambition for a career that she would enjoy. She loved Erik much more than either of these things. And Erik did not want her to leave Dublin.

As soon as he returned from Denmark, where he had spent part of his summer holidays, he asked her to take the Civil Service job and stay with him. For a moment she thought he might ask her to marry him and so fulfil one of her major ambitions at least. But he didn't. He simply pointed out that he had decided last year to stay in Dublin and enroll for a doctorate at Trinity mainly on account of her and that it would be ignoble of her to abandon him now. They were passing by a block of Corporation flats as they had this conversation. The ugly buildings blocked out the light. There was a sour smell in the air: it was the day before bin-day. Nuala felt the pressure of Erik's arm on her waist, a pressure she had not felt all summer while she finished her thesis and deliberated, alone, about her future. His vulnerable, hard-soft, young man's voice moved her. Erik sometimes seemed so tough and independent, and yet he needed her. He needed her and what he said was true.

'All right,' she said. The flats in Oran would probably look like these flats. The smell might be even worse, with all the heat. 'I'll stay.'

The Department of the European Environment was housed in a modern building with a car park in the basement and a great abundance of glossy greenery in the hall. This did something to dispel Nuala's gloom. Exotic, shiny, virulently green plants in fat terracotta pots were something for which she had a soft spot. She relaxed. It would not be so bad after all. There would be the occasional oasis.

Smiling, she gave her name to the ceramic-complexioned girl who sat at the reception desk. The girl did not smile, or ask Nuala to sit down, or advise her what to do. In 1975 Irish civil servants did not feel they had to kowtow to anyone in the world or to make any pretence of good cheer. Nuala should have been pleased by this demonstration of independence and nonconformity but she was not. She would have welcomed a warm word and a bit of information.

The girl phoned somebody and in about ten minutes a steel door slid back and a grey-haired man emerged from it. In warm and reassuring tones he welcomed her to the Civil Service. Then he escorted her up to his office on the fifth floor. This was a little bare hot room. There wasn't a plant in sight, or any other sign of life either. The desk was empty, apart from the telephone and a large diary, open at 10 October. So far the page was blank.

He talked for about two minutes, telling her of the brief history and function of the department in a high thin voice. The HEO would give her some literature which would give her a better idea of what it was all about. He did not explain what the initials HEO meant and Nuala did not ask.

Then he led her to the window and showed her the view. His broad sweeping gestures came as a surprise, suggesting some hidden largesse of spirit. And indeed Nuala found out later that, like many civil servants, he had another life. All his weekends were spent in the Malahide Estuary on a cutter called the *Papillon* and during his summer holidays he crossed the Atlantic, if possible, or else the North Sea, among whose cantankerous waters he found the challenge and peace that eluded him at the office. 'We've a lovely view!' he said.

She looked out. 'It is lovely.'

It was a roofscape. Uneven slated roofs, concrete office blocks, a steeple or two. And, joy of joys, the Peppercannister. On the farther parameters of the scene were the Pidgeon House and the gasometer at Ringsend. 'Oh, it is lovely!' she repeated.

He laughed drily and looked at her in disbelief. And suddenly she realised that he did not like this at all. Men of his age had nothing but distaste for urban decay or urban splendour, and their idea of splendid scenery derived from emigrant love songs and the *Lyrical Ballads*.

Reduced to silence, this man—his name was Muiris—led her to her own room. She supposed it would be like his, and was already planning to introduce a mock castor-oil and maybe a spider plant or two. But in the event she did not have a room of her own at all but a desk in a large chamber shared by six civil servants. The desks were arranged in two rows of three, and in front of them, facing towards the others like a teacher's desk, was the desk of the HEO, who was called Tommy.

Tommy was younger than Muiris and much more lively. He had red hair and a large toothy smile. He quickly dispatched Muiris and introduced Nuala to her colleagues: Sean, a blue-jeaned long-haired lad who was Nuala's coeval, Elizabeth, Paul and Adele, who were CA's (clerical assistants), and Mollie, an older woman who nodded tersely at Nuala and did not shake her hand. Tommy winked at the CAs when this happened and all three sniggered silently.

'How about sitting here, Nuala?' Tommy motioned her towards a desk in the middle of one of the rows. Hurriedly he tidied away a few odds and ends that were lying on it. 'You'll be comfy here.' She sat down and put her bag on the desk. Then she put it on the floor. She stared at Tommy.

'Here!' he said, handing her about six leaflets. 'You can read those for today. Take your time. Settle in. Next week we'll start thinking about what you should be doing. OK?'

CHAPTER TWO

When the day was at last over Nuala ran
through the streets, which looked dusty and
weary as they always do at six o clock, to the
Buttery, where she had a brief drink with Erik.
Brief, not because she would not have willingly
extended it into a night-long session, but
because he was anxious to get back to the
library. Besides, his interest in her newest
experiences was minimal. He did not seem to
understand what she was talking about when
she said it had been difficult to get through the
day with nothing to do except read six
brochures, each containing about ten lines of
text. When she named Tommy and Sean and
Adele his face took on an absent look. Not only
was this sort of job not worth doing, it was not
worth talking about—that was what his
expression, his grunts and silences, told her.
And if she insisted on talking he was not going
to demean himself by listening to her senseless
babble.

At this stage in her life Nuala was so
accustomed to Erik and others not listening to
what she said that this response did not
surprise her. She accepted that what she had to

say was not all that interesting, even though it often seemed fascinating to her: Tommy and Sean and Adele and the others: six new people in one day. The job might be dull but they were not. They were not, really, less interesting than the characters Erik was so busy studying, whose principal virtue seemed to be that they were dead, and that Chaucer—hadn't he been some kind of a civil servant himself?—had gossiped about them in rhyming couplets in the Middle Ages. Ordinary people in the Middle Ages were so fascinating that Erik would devote years of his life to analysing their every fictional utterance. But ordinary people nowadays were not worth a second thought. Would he listen more attentively if she spoke in rhyming couplets? He probably wouldn't even notice.

Diminished instead of uplifted, she left him and walked home.

6 Exeter Place. Shared with her parents and with her sister Mary. Christopher, her brother, was no longer with them but working on building sites in London. He was much cleverer than either of the girls, his mother claimed, but his life had been ruined by television. He had been only four when the Byrnes got their set, soon after the establishment of Telefís Éireann, and so his interest in school learning ended before it began. The girls were already hooked on library books and continued to be good about doing their homework—in between

household chores—even after the arrival of the telly. 'And sure girls are much more biddable than boys anyway,' Mollie Byrne always said. ' He has my heart scalded but they'll do anything you tell them. Girls are easier to rear, everyone knows that.'

6 Exeter Place was a Victorian house on a shabby terrace of similar houses, most long ago abandoned by families and transformed into warrens of flats and bedsitters. Nuala half-liked her home: it had a friendly face, always smiling in the afternoon sun. But old houses, sash windows, noisy plumbing, had not been popular during her formative years, and of course she would not have been living in this house if they had been. All the people she admired lived in semi-detached suburban homes, with Spanish tiles on the roofs, picture windows and lots of red or yellow formica everywhere. The trend was just beginning to change and Nuala was faintly aware of this, but she still had mixed feelings about the house. For her it would always be chockful of associations of cold and frugality. Some sort of self-hatred lay at the foundation of its every plywood embellishment. 'You're fond of yourself, aren't you now!' was one of her mother's favourite taunts. Every brick in the crumbly house had learned this phrase. They jeered at Nuala: 'You're fond of yourself, aren't you now?' Trying to ensure that she never would be.

When she came in at about eight o'clock, her father and mother were sitting on one side of a roaring fire. Opposite them was the roaring television set, which neither of them watched but which they kept on for company all the time anyway. Dessie Byrne was asleep, and Mollie was concentrating deeply on the *Evening Press* crossword.

'Is Erik with you?' She looked up with interest. Usually he was: he liked a cup of cocoa and the nine o'clock news in the comfort of her home before facing the harsher reality of his own.

'No,' said Nuala shortly. She always was short with her mother. It was a type of response she regretted privately but she seemed unable to do anything about it. It had been coming automatically ever since she was about eleven years of age: before that, they had got on very well. She fiddled with the doorknob. 'He's in town,' she added, after a minute, in an grudging and futile effort to be friendly.

'Come over to the fire and warm yourself,' said her mother, immediately sympathetic. The only thing that annoyed Nuala more than her mother's criticisms was her sympathy—which was much more frequent. For some reason which she did not understand, she could cope better with maternal negativism than with maternal love.

'No thanks.' She tried not to snarl but not too hard. 'I'm going to make some tea. Would you like some?'

'No, alannah.' Mollie Byrne actually said 'alannah' as well as other quaint expressions, picked up during her country childhood. Nuala knew she ought to appreciate them. She had studied Hiberno-English dialects, after all, with enthusiasm. But she still wished her mother would speak the monochrome dialect of middle-class Dublin women, which she considered respectable and safe. It was as if Mollie dangled dangerous hooks in her charming terms of endearment and traditional ways of speech. It was one of the few traditional thing left to her, but not an insignificant one. Language was power. Somehow Mollie realised this and Nuala suspected her of using her dialect just to remind people that she came from another kind of world from the one they considered so normal and important. To give them a jolt. 'It's too early for me yet. But you could bring us a cup in an hour or so if you liked.'

Nuala left hastily, not bothering to reply. Not deigning to reply. Really! In an hour or so! As if she had nothing better to do. As if she were always on hand, to make cups of tea on demand.

On hand. On demand.

The girls in the Byrne household had always helped in the house. Another traditional custom faithfully observed: from their earliest years they'd been making—wetting—tea, setting tables, clearing up after meals. When Nuala and her elder sister Mary had been only four and five years old, they had washed dishes twice a day, every day.

'Washing the delph,' that was called. They had had to collect hot water in a bucket from their Aga cooker, which heated but did not distribute water, and pour it into the deep porcelain sink. The sink was yellowed and had spidery brown seams running all over its surface. They were faintly disgusting, like varicose veins. Faintly disgusting also was the grey rag with which each dish had to be wiped before it was stacked on the draining board and immediately, before it had time to drip, snatched away by the girl who was drying. Naturally there had been no cheering hygenic aids: this exercise pre-dated soft sudsy washing-up liquid, disposable wipes, fat comforting rolls of kitchen tissue. In Nuala's memory it had always been carried out on dark interminable winter afternoons and was equated with cold childish hopelessness. The washing up seemed to go on forever.

Their brother had never washed delph. Or done anything else. Mollie had treated him as a special, delicate, important member of the family and everyone else had followed suit unquestioningly. Unresentfully too, since he was, as it happened, a nice boy.

'Doormat,' muttered Nuala to herself, barging into the kitchen.

'What?'

Mary Byrne looked up, her neat brownish face smiling mirthfully. She was one of those people with mirthful eyes, mirthful wrinkles, mirthful teeth. Even her hair curled merrily in laughing black locks over her cheery little head. 'Nothing,' said Nuala in neutral tones. 'I'm going to make coffee. Like some?'

'Oh no, thanks. I'm off coffee.'

Mary's gaze returned to her book, which was a very tiny pale-grey paperback copy of *Stories from the Táin*. The table was littered with large flat volumes, some of which had spilled over on to the floor. An *Old Irish Dictionary*. The *Old Irish Dictionary*, which was available only in about thirty of these unwieldy paperback tomes. Mary's life as a post graduate student in Celtic Studies seemed to consist for the most part in frantic searches through it for the meaning of every Old Irish word she encountered in her slender, unglossed texts. One got the impression from her habits that no Old Irish word ever occurred more than once. She kept the dictionary under her bed as a rule, much to Mollie's chagrin. It was, according to the latter, a rat trap, although so far no rat had made any inroads in it.

'Off coffee?' Nuala turned on the tap and let water splash angrily against the bottom of the electric kettle.

'I'm allergic to caffeine. It gives me pre-menstrual tension.'

'Ahm.' It was typical of Mary to be off caffeine and on pre-menstrual whatever before Nuala had ever even heard of either of them. Mary was always one jump ahead: she'd always been the one to win medals for Irish dancing, to learn to read before anyone else in the class. Plenty of go in her. Bright as a button. Everyone's hopes were pinned on Mary. She was doing a PhD, giving tutorials at the university, forging her way towards some brilliant future in the fast lane. Nuala had it all mapped out already. A fellowship in Canada or some such land of opportunity. A professorship. Brief appearances on television, elucidating knotty problems for the nation. Giving informed witty opinions on books and things. OK, so she'd never actually seen an Old Irish scholar on television. But Mary was different. She'd diversify.

Oh, Nuala had high hopes all right, and with good reason. Everyone knew Mary was clever. Most people knew every mark she'd got in every exam. she'd ever done, from the Primary to the BA. Mollie Byrne had been generous with such information. As PR agent for Mary you could not have found anyone better, in spite of Mollie's private opinion that girls were the inferior sex. But Nuala knew more about Mary than her examination results could tell you. More than Mary knew about herself. Mary, Nuala knew, was pushy. Somehow Mollie's putdowns had made no impression on her. She had tossed them aside, laughing. Her unshakable self-confidence thrived on opposition. Mary firmly believed, always, in any company, that she was the most intelligent person in the room. This attitude informed all her opinions and plans. Given that she was in fact not unintelligent, had a good figure and a nice face, she was likely to succeed.

'I'll have some orange juice with hot water,' Mary said, and Nuala made her some, happy, in this instance, to play the maid. Then she sat down on the floor, placing her mug on a pile of volumes of the dictionary, which were already stained with coffee, ketchup, wine and lipstick.

'So how was it?' asked Mary, in her warm concerned voice. She had one of those voices, too, that always sounds interested and interesting.

'Boring as hell,' said Nuala, wondering if it were really true. Could you be sure that it was boring, or that it was just something about you that was wrong, that was the million dollar question.

'I suppose so,' Mary agreed sympathetically. 'Is there any hope, would you say?'

'No I wouldn't say so.' Nuala felt happy; at last she was getting a chance to complain. She loved grumbling and invariably felt good after a long whining-session. Luckily she belonged to a generation which permitted this and did not insist on relentless positive thinking. 'I'm pretty sure that it won't get better. It's just awful, it's unbelievable.'

'Funny how so many people do it, isn't it? It's the money of course.'

'The money isn't all that great.'

Nuala lied. The money was marvellous. Astronomical salaries, people were paid, considering what they had to do for them. Simply be present in a particular place for forty hours a week. Well. It would have been better, much better, if you could do your forty hours at one stretch and get them over with.

'You haven't got any yet, though, have you?' What was she going to do, ask for the loan of a few quid? You couldn't be sure with these post-grad types. Artists. Intellectuals. Always ready to scrounge off the employed.

'No. You have to work a week first.'

'I'd like the money, I must admit.' Mary sipped her nauseous mixture thoughtfully. 'To buy things.'

'You seem to manage well enough without it.'

'Do I? I want all sorts of things. You can't imagine!' Her face grew dreamy, then avaricious. 'Things that money can buy. Holidays. A car. Clothes.'

Mary was fond of clothes. This was her single weakness, that she considered clothes important, and that she considered herself an excellent model for them. Possibly she was right in that; her looks were not remarkable.

'Youse are no ile paintins,' Mollie had said to Mary and Nuala, in one of her maternal tête-à-têtes. Beauty had not been top of the agenda when her attitudes had been formed. As in a certain type of school, the type of school the Byrnes had gone to, beautiful girls were looked upon with distrust. Attractiveness was dangerous. The fact was that Mary, although not stricty beautiful, would have made an admirable subject for an oil or any type of painting—excluding, of course, the kind with which the walls of the Byrne house were adorned, that is, oleographs of the Little Flower and the Sacred Heart, a calendar from the local garage showing buxom blondes in bikinis and one exceptionally gloomy painting of the Crucifixion, depicting faces of the most forlorn and abject misery overlaid with bottle-green paint. But in cheerful acrylics or delicate watercolours Mary would have looked most appropriate, with her dark hair and red mouth. And her slim energetic figure made her an ideal clothes-horse. It was natural that she would want more than the jeans and jumpers she was able to afford on her small scholarship.

'The price is high,' Nuala sighed. How high she did not yet know. 'There's more to life than clothes and holidays.'

'Is there?'

'You know there is. Why pretend?' Nuala felt her irritation rise again.

'I'm not pretending. I actually don't know.'

'You sit here reading Old Irish and you say that! I mean…well you probably take it all for granted. Stimulation and fulfilment. And so on.'

'There must be some of that even in the Civil Service.'

'Maybe.' Nuala doubted it. 'But it certainly lacks…a spiritual dimension, I suppose, is what I mean.'

'Who needs a spiritual dimension?'

For someone who had been brought up in a house filled with oleographs of the Sacred Heart and all that goes with them, this was a surprising question, Nuala thought. It suggested that in the deepest as well as the most superficial ways Mary was different from her. Occasionally it did seem that her success in life was due to her carelessness about it. She wasn't concerned, one way or the other, about what happened to her. So good things happened.

Nuala felt depressed again, at her new discovery. That she needed a spiritual dimension and that there wasn't one in her job or in most other jobs. Her mind, as it was wont to do when saddened by any particular thing, wandered in the direction of other unhappy phenomena. Misery likes bedfellows. Her thoughts returned to the brown dull shades of the Buttery, to the image of Erik scowling at her in its noisy shadows, and from there to the greyness of the Department of the European

35

Environment. She wanted to cry, and in case that should happen she drank her tea quickly and brought the cup to the scullery.

'How is Erik?' asked Mary, changing the subject, not very successfully.

'He's OK. How is Brendan?' countered Nuala. How is Erik, how is Brendan? How is Tom, Dick, Harry? This was a loaded question. Girls asked it of each other regularly, and not because they were interested in the health and wellbeing of each other's boyfriends. What they were interested in was, if they were kind, bolstering the confidence of the questioned girl, and if they were nasty, finding out if the relationship were still on. Girls, it seemed, almost always wanted relationships with boys to last for ever and ever, differing markedly from boys, men and even wives in this crucial respect, much to their own ultimate discomfort and misery.

'Oh Brendan!' Mary laughed a brittle laugh. 'We broke up a month ago, didn't you know?'

'No.'

Nuala could not think of anything further to say. What she wanted to ask was, who broke it off? But it would be impolite to ask, and anyway Mary would say it was mutual. Girls always did, if they were mature and sensible, as Mary was. Silly girls broke down and wept and told you the whole sorry tale. They didn't seem to worry about whether you were interested, whether you were a good listener or not. All they wanted to do was spill the beans into any container that made itself, however inadvertently, available.

Mary answered the unspoken question anyhow.

'I broke it off. At the beginning of September. I just couldn't take it any more.'

'The beginning of September?' Nuala was shocked. Just before his final Med. Relationships between men and women were not bound by the usual rules of civilised social intercourse. Every fool accepted that. But there were limits to the 'All's fair. . .' rule. Even the IRA called a truce at Christmas. And in a student's life final examinations were more significant than Christmas.

'I know!' Mary sighed briefly. 'People think I'm callous and all that.' Mary always used qualifying phrases when covering up her sins. Her 'all thats' implied that the people in question were dopes who didn't know the half of it. 'But I really couldn't hold out one minute longer and anyway I think it was a good time to break it off. He'd so much to do that he couldn't even think about it then.'

'Maybe you're right,' nodded Nuala. What she thought was: so that's why Brendan got a pass degree. He'd never been top of the class, but he'd always come fairly close—otherwise Mary would not have looked twice at him. So it had been a surprise to find his name down at the bottom with the also rans. Poor old

Brendan. He'd been so nice. Was still so nice. Too nice, probably. Girls like Mary never went for really nice men. Nuala didn't either. 'Is there someone else?'

She guessed that there would be. Mary was too mercenary to give up one man if there were not another hovering in the wings. Civilised men in Dublin were valuable commodities. It was like Enid Blyton books in the kids section of the public library. You never returned one to the librarian: you swapped it first for a Blyton book you hadn't read. In the grown-up world, you didn't give up one job until you'd got an alternative. The same was true of an eligible man. It was a sellers' market, as far as suitable men and jobs and Enid Blyton books were concerned. Suitable women, educational courses—like books by Charles Dickens—were different, and could be abandoned at will without great risk. There were always lots of them around.

'Oh, there is someone.' Mary smiled coyly, and began to thumb frantically through a volume marked 'C'.

CHAPTER THREE

When Nuala had expressed scepticism and scorn for her sister's materialistic ambitions she was not being altogether just or honest with herself. Because the truth was that she herself, in spite of her half-realized desire for something spiritual, was also very interested in the things money can buy. And she had various plans for uses to which her new salary could be put.

One of her deep-seated frivolous desires was a wish to ride a horse. She decided to gratify this craving almost as soon as she received her first pay-cheque. This was in spite of her guilty fear of spending any money she earned, in case she should suddenly be obliged to resign from her job. Already after two weeks she had confronted the ironic truth about her position: the safe secure job held no security or safety for her, since she could not trust herself to stay in it. Probably—but how could she be sure? — there would have been more security in any scrap of a job that was to her taste, or even in no job at all. As it was, she was in limbo. However, to take a riding lesson was not to mortgage her entire future, so she went ahead and did it. Since childhood she had been reading about girls who loved ponies, girls who did ballet-dancing, girls who ice-skated their way to fame and fortune. Girls who went to Malory Towers. Her entire childhood, like that of most Irish children, or most children anywhere, had been lived against this mental backdrop of a glamorous alternative, sprinkled with ice-skates and ballet-slippers and shining saddles. A fantasy world, but one which was usually presented in a realistic mode, so that Nuala believed that other ideal world existed and that it was through sheer bad luck that she was not the real life heroine of some biography called *Dream of Sadler's Wells* or *Pony Girl*.

She booked two lessons, one for her and one for Erik, who was less reluctant than might have been expected to participate in the new enterprise and who accompanied her under barely token protest on the 44 bus to Sandyford one Saturday towards the end of October. Erik had never ridden but he was under the spell of JP Dunleavy, and the potion included a sort of turf-aphrodisiac (among others).

They got off the bus at the cross of Sandyford and then walked for half a mile along a country lane to the stables, Rickett's Lodge. She felt pleased with herself as she trotted along. Here they were, hardly on the outskirts of the city but already in the middle of a real settled rural landscape. A few minutes behind the estates sprawled and below them

Dublin squatted like a nuclear toadstool, but on this lane, Rocky Mountain Lane, were farmhouses and fields that looked as if they could produce real vegetables and potatoes and corn for real people, the delightful people who inhabited the farmhouses, who owned the chickens, black and brown and red, which ran around the yards, who mended, not too often, the barbed wire fences. Some of the fields were, joy of joys, under stubble, and the lane was scattered with red leaves which beech trees and sycamores had considerately dropped. It was a lovely autumn day, a crunchy wholenut sort of day, and as Nuala squashed leaf after leaf under her desert-booted feet she was pleasantly conscious of her embarkation on a crunchy wholenut type of adventure.

Erik also appreciated all this but he did not express his sentiments. He never did, as far as nature was concerned, as far as scenery was concerned, although he loved them as much as she did. It was just that he found beauty embarrassing, as embarrassing as, say, religion. And also that he had a natural terseness, which he claimed to have inherited from his long line of puritan ancestors.

Erik was an atheistic Danish Lutheran. (Thus he referred to himself, and such indeed he was.) Nuala had picked him up, literally, in the canteen in Fairfield, about a year and a half before, where she had found him asleep at a table, slumped over a plate of cold chips and tomato ketchup. One of his hands stretched across the grey formica table and the other dangled towards the floor, retaining, miraculously, a tentative grip on a fat book, Robinson's edition of the works of Chaucer. Nuala, who had believed herself to be acquainted with every student of Middle English in Fairfield, wondered who he was, since she had never seen him before. And, since he looked so pathetic and helpless, sleeping in the clangorous canteen in the middle of the day, and since he also looked, even in that undignified position, remarkably handsome, she shook him and woke him up.

He was, she learned quickly, handsome and pathetic and helpless all at once, all the time. And the truth is that she took advantage of the latter weaknesses and bound him to her by assisting him to alternative moods and modes of being.

Then again, one could say that he had free will (although one cannot be sure how much of this an atheistic Danish Lutheran believes he possesses). He need not have succumbed so easily. But few men would have been able to resist Nuala's kindness and efforts, and her general *savoir faire*, and few would have been able to resist her deadly efficiency. In a matter of months he was cured.

Of what, one might ask? As she got to know him the nature of Erik's problems had quickly become apparent to Nuala. He was a research student at Trinity, working on a poem by Geoffrey Chaucer, 'The Friar's Tale'. He had been there for six months. But he was not settling in. Coming as it did directly on the heels of his undergraduate course at the University of Copenhagen, where he had been a star student and the recipient of all manner of plaudits, the indifference with which students at Irish universities were regarded by their teachers had propelled him into a state of acute depression. He had begun to suspect that he might not, after all, be the cleverest boy in the world. This was worrying, and the worry gnawed at him night and day, the more so because he lived in a truly horrible damp bedsitter off Wicklow Street, and ate nothing but cans of baked beans and pints of milk and the occasional chip in Fairfield. The food in the Buttery he could not stomach at all.

He'd decided to drop out of college. He wanted to be a poet, and for some reason or other, to do with his Danishness or atheism or Protestantism, he believed that one had to concentrate entirely on whatever one was doing. The concept of part-time writing was simply alien to his way of thinking. He came from a culture of specialists such as Ireland could not afford. It was all or nothing. His plan was to go back to Denmark and become a poet. This was problem number one. In addition, he had just gone through three months of believing he was Jesus Christ, as residents of lanes off Wicklow Street, if they come from rich Danish families, probably often do. Luckily the only person to whom he'd confided this information, apart from Nuala, was the college psychiatrist, a fat paternal man who'd advised him to go to the Merriman Summer School and find a girl. Since it was November Erik had gone to the Merriman Winter School instead, and it had depressed him even more than Dublin or Ireland or Trinity. There had been no girls, only gangs of middle-aged men drinking Guinness and whiskey all day and all night, and lectures that were badly attended and poorly delivered, and a very chilly room in a bungalow on the outskirts of Milltown Malbay, a place which is not at its best in late November. The first thing he'd done when he'd come home was to try to commit suicide by putting his head in the oven. But the gas had run out, as it frequently did. The landlord was an unusually mean man, even by landlordly standards, and he'd rigged the meter. And Erik couldn't find another tenpence piece. Anyway with that meter it would have taken about ten pounds to do yourself in. In fact you couldn't do it, unless you had an accomplice to put tenpenny pieces into the meter every couple of seconds, and then it wouldn't have been suicide.

What a bloody awful country! So Erik had lived, to wander around Dublin and write poems, and wonder if he shouldn't write to his mother instead, and ask for the fare home.

From this mess Nuala rescued him.

No wonder he loved her.

His salvation had been achieved, however, with little active effort on her part; all she had done was encourage him to talk. Unlike the young people with whom Nuala was best acquainted, who were at all times prepared to bare their souls to any listener, who indeed gloried in that exercise, Erik was genuinely reserved. It seemed that he had scarcely opened his mouth since his arrival in Ireland. He claimed that this was owing to his suspicion that nobody was interested in anything he had to say, and also that they distrusted his accent, which was chiefly characterised by a strange Danish phonological habit known as the glottal stop. This made him appear to be hiccupping all the time. Moreover when he first spoke to her he used an exceptionally thin dry voice. It was almost cracking, and it seemed to her that his larynx had dehydrated from lack of practice, although this is hardly a physical possibility. But very soon his tone deepened and matured, and she found that she had released to the world a large booming intensely masculine tenor, much to her own gratification, since she had a penchant for just such voices. Indeed it is not going too far to say that she had sometimes fallen for a man on account of his voice alone.

That was not why she fell in love with Erik,

45

or not the only reason. The main factor which attracted her was his appearance. In a way she had loved him at first sight, from the moment she caught a glimpse of his delicious fair hair, falling in a winsome Ampleforth lock across his forehead as it rested on a paper serviette. He did not have a stereotypical public school physique, apart from his hair. His chin, for instance, was strong, even stubborn, and his skin was close-pored and sallow so that he was tanned even in winter. He had regular, chiselled features, deep brown eyes, and a body which Nuala likened, unoriginally, to that of a Greek god or an Olympic athlete, depending on her mood. In his day he had in fact been an athlete, and had taken a bronze for Denmark in the 200 metres freestyle in the 1972 Olympics. But he had relinquished swimming in favour of medieval literature—a sacrifice which no doubt made him unique in the modern world. Since coming to Ireland he had not swum a stroke, being under the impression that there were no swimming pools in Dublin. One of Nuala's early offices had been to guide him to Tara Street, and one of her first pleasures to watch him dive like a tern from the side of the pool into the brilliant chlorine-blue waters of Dublin's oldest bath and emerge some seconds later, his hair the colour of kelp and water glittering on his golden skin.

Besides his looks, he was remarkably attractive on account of his interest in literature, and especially in Old English literature. Men studying this subject were rarer than gold-dust. It was rumoured that a boy had taken Old English in 1970 but he had been gay. Nuala's class, and all the classes above and below within predatory range, had been exclusively female in composition. She'd discovered this when she'd been in one of them for two months, when it was too late to change to something else, like history or Irish, which men seemed to like. As it turned out, there had been a pleasant gemütlichkeit in belonging to the all-girl class, as there must have been in those female colleges in America and Oxford before they went co-ed and fell into men's hands. But the cosiness did not help one find a mate. Nuala knew, of course, theoretically, that somewhere in the world men did—or rather read, as they would express it in those exotic places—Old English. The exclusively male teaching staff of the Old English department suggested that this must be so. But although logic indicated that these shy middle-aged men, men like Robin Allgood, had once been shy young men, Nuala's intuitive feeling about them was that they had emerged from some kind of middle-earth fully grown, wearing black gowns and clutching degrees from Oxford in one pale hand and aromatic pipes in the other, to take up their destined quarters in the little grey cells of Fairfield and teach Old English to modern Irish girls.

And now. Here was a real living young man who studied that subject. And moreover he was not a weed but athletic and good-looking. And moreover he was a poet.

At least, he was a poet when Nuala met him. But she had disliked his poems, which were not the earthy neo-Whitman stuff she favoured, but rather intellectual bony poems. Rather terse and spare, in the manner of Icelandic sagas. Perhaps Scandinavian literature was like that. She wasn't familiar with it, apart from its earliest manifestations in Old Norse prose. That sort of thing, she felt, was fine in sagas. Or furniture. Erik's poems reminded her of Swedish armchairs, all sharp structure, not much padding. Nice to look at, but ...She had pretended to admire the poems, however, and advised Erik to send them to a literary journal she knew of and to enclose a stamped addressed envelope for reply. He had been piqued at the latter suggestion, although not at the former. He despatched his poems with a carefully worded letter of introduction typed on thick cream paper, and without a stamped addressed envelope.

He never heard from the journal.

That was the end of his career as a poet and the beginning of his affair with Nuala. The encouragement to send off the poems predisposed him to love, the failure of the editor to respond turned the scales; three weeks after he had sent off the poems, he kissed her one night in the hallway of 6 Exeter Place, just before he left to go to his new flat. The kiss was firm and pleasant, but afterwards he laughed to himself in a somewhat disquieting way. Nuala knew better than to take umbrage and inquire into the motivation for the laugh. She was still nursing him; he was still in a vulnerable condition; any rocking of the boat could have plummeted him back to the abyss of silence and sullen depression from which he'd come. So she took the kiss for what it was worth, and from there on it had been relatively plain sailing. They had by now enjoyed a relationship for more than a year. They had shared interests in matters to do with literature and the outdoor life and had become what is known as a popular couple. Erik was a hit in Fairfield, where he was a touch of class, an exotic rarity: an intelligent literate young man with a nice face and body.

By now, Erik had developed so well that he was also popular on his own account; with his background and looks, it required only a modicum of effort on his part to win interesting friends and innumerable invitations. He had a large selection of followers now whom Nuala did not even know. They were going to visit one of these people tonight, after the riding lesson. The person—her name was Melissa—was throwing a party in her flat in Monkstown.

But now they had arrived at Rickett's Lodge.

They were opening the five-barred gate. They were walking into the mucky yard. They found themselves in a cobbled enclosure surrounded by an assortment of sheds and barns, and permeated by a smell and aura of horses, although not a single living creature, equine or human, was to be seen. Nuala felt her heart sink momentarily: she had come at the wrong time; it was the wrong place; there were no horses at this place. She thought. Such moments of uncertainty were becoming frequent with her of late. A year earlier she had had no doubts. Now—since joining the Civil Service—the world was becoming increasingly unpredictable. The most horrible things could happen to her, in spite of her best efforts. But her fears were as usual pointless, because in less than five minutes a line of horses ambled into the yard and stood with their backs to the wall, giving Nuala and Erik sly corner-boy glances, as if they resented their existence.

Nuala and Erik nosed around diffidently, examining the horses from a safe distance, going into a shed and looking with a show of great interest at the perfectly ordinary harnasses and saddles which were hanging there, handling them with more courage than they had exhibited with the horses. They were more inquisitive than was strictly polite, because they sensed they were under observation and they wanted to display a self-confidence with neither of them felt: Nuala, because she was so totally out of her element, Erik because, although he came from a background which should have filled him with self-assuredness, had very little when it came to the crunch.

Eventually, after ten more minutes, the one who had been watching emerged from a door at the opposite side of the yard, and shouted in a loud masculine voice: 'Hey there, can I help you? Hey! Hey!'

They jumped out of their anoraks.

The voice emanated from a minute bandy-legged figure, dressed in a tattered brown riding cap, Aran jumper and muddy fawn breeches. It was a female figure, that of Miss Bess Burton, who owned the stables. She had, as well as her gruff voice and tatty clothes, an authentic Anglo-Irish accent, and Nuala's heart warmed to her, even though she recognised instantly the rude, nasty, malicious, mean side of Miss Bess Burton's character. It didn't matter; what was important was that she represented the type of character who was so popular in the novels that Nuala and everyone else was reading at the moment, their most endearing stereotype, the darling of feminists: the eccentric maiden aunt. Shut up in the west wing or shut up in the stable or not shut up at all but flung out on to the dungheap of the non-Anglo-Irish world, the mire of native rusticity, to earn a living selling potted plants or teaching townies to ride, subsisting on a diet of lettuce

and tomatoes in summer, potatoes in winter,
their only solace the odd Baby Power or baby
bottle of vanilla essence.

Miss Burton blew a whistle. Immediately
half a dozen or more girls, aged about sixteen,
emerged from stalls and stables, barns and
holes in the wall. They set to work and after
what seemed a long time to Nuala all the
horses were standing in the yard, saddled and
bridled and ready to go. Miss Burton gave
Nuala a fat old mare called Strawberry and
Erik a sprightly chestnut by the name of Rock.

The ride went well for Erik, who had never
been on a horse before. He had a good seat,
Miss Burton said, and he himself remarked that
it was like riding a bicycle. All the little girls
laughed when he said this. They laughed at
every remark he made, all afternoon, and one
in particular, slightly older than the others and
very attractive, rode alongside him and made
one or two jokes herself. Her name was
Vogue—Vogue is a Wexford saint but Erik and
Nuala did not know this, and took it that she
had been called after a woman's magazine. She
looked as if she might have been.

Erik had plenty of opportunity to make
Vogue's acquaintance, since Nuala was hardly
ever at his side. Strawberry was old, but not as
gentle as Miss Burton had implied. First she
was stubborn and would not keep up with the
troop.

'Kick her!' Miss Burton ordered. 'Kick her

properly!'

Obediently Nuala kicked. Then when Strawberry started to trot she pulled on the reins, terrified, to slow her down. Whereupon Mollie stood still and refused to move.

'Kick her!' shouted Miss Burton. 'You're slowing everyone down. Let her know that you are in control. Otherwise she'll take advantage of you.'

Strawberry was an experienced hack and no amount of kicking deceived her. She knew who was in control and it was not Nuala. She seemed to take a malicious delight in this, and began to play up. Sometimes she stood still and refused to move. Then she trotted smartly along and caught up with the troop. Then, just as Nuala was catching her breath and beginning to feel that she would walk, unalarmingly, with the other horses, she slowed down again. Miss Burton screamed at both of them all the time. In the end Strawberry bolted, and shot across a road, across a ditch and up a steep hill towards an eight-foot wall with Nuala clinging on desperately and realising that in spite of everything that was wrong with her life she was not ready to die. Not yet.

At the wall Strawberry stopped. Nuala slid off her back. Her whole body was shaking and she could hardly walk. But she led Strawberry by the reins back to the bottom of the hill where the others waited and watched.

'She gave you a good run for your money in the end,' said Miss Burton.

'Are you all right?' asked Erik. But his voice was not kind. It was tight and ashamed. She had disgraced him in front of the little girls, who were all experts in the saddle. She was older than them and not as pretty and not as neatly turned out, and she had to go and make a show of herself. Just like her!

CHAPTER FOUR

Erik and Nuala were cool with one another on the way home from Sandyford but their antagonism did not reach crisis-point. Under different circumstances they would have had a stormy row; their relationship had reached a stage where loud nerve-wracking quarrels were commonplace. The control which Nuala had possessed in the delicate early days she had relinquished completely; now she was always ready to fly into a rage upon the slightest provocation. What prevented it happening on this occasion was lack of time.

The plan was that they should proceed to Melissa's party under their own steam; this was Erik's idea. It had seemed sensible to Nuala when he'd first suggested it, on account of the logistics of clothes-changing, but when the moment of parting arrived she felt annoyed and even tearful. To leave Erik even for an hour was becoming increasingly difficult; she was afraid that if she took her eyes off him he would disappear. Although in fact what seemed in fact to happen was the opposite. As soon as he took his eyes off her, she ceased to exist. She had become dependent on him not only for her happiness—odd, since she was almost always unhappy—but for her being. Without him she felt like nothing.

The journey to the party, in a half-empty bus rattling along suburban roads, felt perilous. The other passengers, who included many couples, were an affront to her partnerless state. The darkness surrounding the lighted bus seemed to her a great dangerous void, a metaphor for the emptiness of the infinite world-without-Erik which she now feared more than anything. Her fear was almost at the level of a phobia, and in fact she was suffering from one, although she did not know it. Since she had not recognised it as a phobia she had never got around to asking herself what she was afraid of. All she knew was that since the end of the summer and the start of the new job, this fear had become stronger than it had ever been before.

She felt better with her feet on the ground and her eyes seeking the name of the square on which Melissa lived: Eaton Square. The cold air on her face gave her pleasure and the gemlike orange streetlamps, the windows of drawing rooms which gleamed as welcoming lanterns in the black pool of the night cheered her up. She was a brisk walker and enjoyed the exercise, as well as the feeling of her ˙thick silky skirt brushing against her purposefully striding legs.

The flat she found without difficulty, which was also gratifying, since the area was unfamiliar to her. Melissa opened the door and greeted her with effusion; her manners were open and charming in a way which Nuala considered to be typical of New Yorkers, although Melissa was the only New Yorker she had ever met in the flesh.

'Isn't Erik with you? Not yet? Well never mind, you come right along with me, honey, and enjoy the party!'

She took Nuala's hand, much to the latter's appreciation, and led her along an elegant hall and downstairs to a large softly-lit room. Nuala noted instantly the stone-tiled floor, the timbered ceiling, the modern Swedish furniture. She was impressed. Melissa was obviously rich. Erik had told her she was on a Fulbright. Now she understood what that meant.

Melissa herself looked like any American post-graduate student of the time. She was tall and pretty, with especially pretty large teeth and a wide smile. Her clothes, on this occasion a printed smock, midnight blue with tiny red flowers, worn with heavy fisherman's socks and clogs, were standard, as were the little granny spectacles which lent a dotty charm to her face, as they were intended to. The only truly exceptional thing about her looks was her hair. Long hair had been in fashion for about five or six years in Ireland: it was just on the way out, in fact, but many girls, including Nuala, wore their hair to their shoulders.

Melissa, however, had gone the whole hog, and her rough fairish locks extended to her bottom, when plaited in their thick Rapunzel braid. Loose, which it never was under normal circumstances, it must have come to her knees. But, of course, hair was free. You could not have guessed that Melissa was better off than everyone else just by looking at her. Only by visiting her flat could you perceive this fact, which was of great interest to Nuala, as it would have been to any Upwardly Socially Mobile Person.

'Look, here's the wine and here's the food. Why don't you just take one of these glasses here...' Melissa stuck a goblet of red into Nuala's hand. 'And make yourself at home.'

She smiled and disappeared to answer another ring at the door.

Perhaps it's Erik, Nuala thought optimistically, sipping the wine, which was all right, and surveying the room. Among the groups of drinking, talking people she did not see one face that she recognised, at first. Then she noticed a woman called Annie Harrison whom she had met in Trinity. She went up to her and sat down beside her on a white leather sofa. Annie said hello and continued her conversation with the man seated on the other side of her, a rather middle-aged-looking person dressed in grey trousers and a sweater of some nondescript colour which could not be specified in the candlelit room. In spite of his grocer's assistant appearance, he turned out to be a student of Old English, just like Erik. And Annie. And most of the people at this party. They were talking, not about *Beowulf* or 'The Seafarer' or even about Chaucer—and how could one talk about these things?—but about members of staff in the department of English. Not only the contents of their courses, the style of their teaching, their personalities as lecturers, were of interest to their post-graduate students, but every tiny detail of their private lives as well.

'Ken has turquoise wallpaper in his dining room. It's stunning. You'd never think it would work but it does.'

'Della has good taste obviously!' Colm, the grocer's assistant, had never been to Ken's house, as Annie knew.

'Yes, she does.' Della was, of course, Ken's wife. 'The house is really very attractive, and I suppose that's her imput. I mean I can't imagine Ken caring much about the house, can you?'

Hilarious laughter. Honk honk, went Annie. What big teeth you have Annie, thought Nuala. Big but not beautiful, not like Melissa's. Strawberry's face flitted across the surface of her mind, snarling vindictively.

'No. I can't imagine him being interested in anything except Arthurian romance. He never thinks about anything else.'

Did this mean that he never talked about

anything else either? Nuala supposed so. She, like Annie and Colm, had always assumed that her teachers had continuous deep fascinating conversations with other interested parties about various aspects of language and literature. But when she had been an undergraduate she had naïvely assumed that people like Colm and Annie would have been having such conversations too. By now she knew that post-graduates never talked about anything but other people, and almost all conversation seemed to remain at the level of gossip, or, at best, popular psychological analysis of personalities, especially the personalities of lecturers and professors whom they were anxious to impress, initially, and then replace. Perhaps Ken talked mainly about interior decors and his colleagues, just like everyone else?

'Yeah, Della's a really nice woman. I like her. I don't know how she keeps sane, with those kids. God, I'd go round the bend if I were her. And the house...she dresses badly, though, I must say. That makes one wonder, doesn't it? I mean, could someone who dresses like Della dresses design a nice dining room?'

Girl students were not keen on lecturers having wives. They tried to keep them away from parties, by claiming, correctly but not very kindly, that they were not part of the college life, and by not inviting them. It wasn't that the girl students wanted to develop close relationships with the lecturers, start affairs with them or anything. But they wanted to show off to them and it was easier to do this if their wives were not around.

Nuala left them to ponder the question of Della's aesthetic sense, and, emboldened by the wine, which she had managed to drain in less than five minutes, made her way across to the table. It was laden with French rolls and camembert, and some bowls of something that looked like the pupils of tiny birds eyes. She tasted a little of the latter, didn't like it (it tasted like eyes, too), took a chunk of bread and some cheese, and stood there eating them. Eventually someone else came up to feed, as she had known they would.

He stood beside her, eating spoonfuls of the eyes.

'I love caviar,' he said in apologetic tones, having observed Nuala observing him.

'Mmm, me too,' she said. Another one of life's disappointments. And where was Erik?

'Hey, don't I knew you from somewhere? Are you one of the Hogans of Foxrock?'

'My name is Nuala Byrne,' said Nuala, with artful simplicity.

'You look so like someone I know.'

'Oh, I just have one of those faces.'

'Mmm.' Did not commit himself. 'Look, would you like some of this? I don't want to scoff the lot before anyone gets a look in.'

'Thanks, I'd love some.' Nuala let him pass

her a spoon, and then let him put the spoon in her mouth. 'Nyum nyum!' she said. 'Now I think I'll get some more wine. What are you having?'

'White.'

'The red's better.'

'Red.'

They sat down on a large yellow beanbag. Paddy Lynch was his name. He lived in Foxrock himself, and was a worker, not a student. Nuala felt relieved at that; she was ashamed to be an employed person among so many students and particularly to be employed as she was, in the most unglamorous of occupations. When Paddy told her that he was a civil servant too, she felt an enormous surge of relief.

'I don't believe it. Which department?'

'Education. I work in the City Library actually.'

'Oh.' Deflation. 'That's not quite the same thing, is it?'

'We are civil servants. And it is pretty awful, if that's what you mean.'

'That's what I mean. If it's awful why are you doing it?'

'I got the job. They're employing lots of graduates in the Civil Service now, to keep the unemployment figures down—that's how you've got your job. I know heaps of MAs in English Lit and so on who are in the Department of Agriculture and the Department of Industry and Commerce and all the rest of them. '

'Isn't that tragic? I think its tragic.'

'Oh, I don't know.' Paddy Lynch had a round soft face and a fluffy brown beard. His eyes smiled gently all the time, or looked as if they did, and he wore soft brown tweed pants and an Aran jumper. His appearance suggested that he was of easygoing disposition. 'It's what you make of it, I suppose, isn't it?'

'That's my problem, I just don't know.'

'The mind is its own place and in itself/can make a Heaven of Hell, a Hell of Heaven.'

'I always think he's referring to prison when he's saying that. I can't get it into my head that it's actually about hell and heaven, literally. And sometimes I think I'd rather be in prison than in the Civil Service.'

'Why?'

'I don't know really, I suppose because I think I'd have more time to myself. To do my own thing. And that I'd get out eventually.'

'But you are out. And you wouldn't have time to yourself in prison; you'd be sewing mailbags or picking oakum or something like that.'

'I think, sometimes—am I crazy?—that sewing mailbags would be preferable to what I'm doing.'

'Which is?'

'Well, nothing, mainly. Messing around. Everything seems to take about five minutes to do, and you're supposed to make it last for two days.'

'Oh yeah. That's what happened when they overstaffed. There is nothing to do, actually. But if you hang in there for a few years there probably will be. This trend will change eventually.'

'You're right.' Nuala felt cheerful again. She had totally forgotten Erik, and had forgotten that he was the reason she was in the Civil Service to begin with.

'Let's drink to that!'

They drank to it, and afterwards, since people had begun to dance, they danced too. Nuala did not consider the state of her emotions, but had she done so she might have been surprised to find that, whereas some hours earlier she had felt as if her right arm had been cut off because Erik had gone to his flat to dress for the party, she now was oblivious of the fact that he had not yet arrived, although the evening was wearing on and some people—not many—had already gone home. Erik hadn't come but she was happy anyway. Paddy was not as attractive as Erik. She knew instinctively that she would never be in love with him. But he spoke her language. He listened to what she was saying and understood what it was about. And what he said himself made more sense to her than most things she heard. Paddy was the sort of person she could do with in her life as a friend.

While she was dancing with Paddy, Colm, the Old English student she had met initially, came up and said, 'Excuse me!' to him with an exaggerated bow, and whisked Nuala off with surprising panache. He was very drunk.

'Annie's been telling me you're Mary Byrne's sister?'

'Yes. That's right.'

'I know Mary very well. You're not a bit like her. Yeah, I know Mary. She was going out with my brother for a while.'

'Oh?' Nuala felt panic.

'Brendan.'

'Oh yeah. I know Brendan. How is he? I haven't seen him in an age.'

'He's all right. He's broken up with Mary, you know. I thought it was very sad. They were a lovely couple. Luverly.'

'I liked Brendan very much.'

'The salt of the earth. Ah, Mary doesn't know what's good for her. I mean, all girls are attracted to their teachers, we all know that. But she's taking it too far.'

'What do you mean?'

'That's the question, isn't it? What do I mean, what do I mean? Ah sure maybe I don't know what I mean myself.'

He steered her over to the corner where Paddy was and left her there.

'Drunken fool!' she said, since she was slightly inebriated herself.

'Oh yes, obviously,' Paddy smiled. He was

talking to Robin Allgood, who had materialised at the party rather late. Nuala nodded to him and did not smile, since she was feeling cross again.

'I'm going home,' she said. 'It's late, I'll miss my bus.'

'You have missed it; it's almost one o clock.' Paddy smiled at her. 'I'll give you a lift. Where is it you live?'

She told him.

'On my way. Hang on a minute, will you, till I finish this. Then we'll go.'

Nuala went to get her coat from the bedroom where Melissa had flung all of them on to her big bed. She sat at the dressing table and looked at her face in the mirror. Her skin was pale. Well, that was natural, it was so late. Her eyes had a dry tired look, and her hair, which she had washed hurriedly just before coming out, lay flat and lifeless against her cheeks. She believed its bright auburn colour was fading; already it showed hints of brown. In the comfortable cosy bedroom, with its rosy wallpaper and floral bedspread, its rose-shaded lamps everywhere but over the mirror, where you'd need one, Nuala looked out of place. A weary drudge. A menial minion in a world of ease and leisure. Melissa's world.

She thought of Victorian seamstresses, working seventeen hours a day in cramped rooms. She thought of Victorian chimney-sweeps, spending their childhoods in black sooty furnaces. She thought of slaves picking cotton in Kentucky fields.

And she felt like them.

CHAPTER FIVE

When Erik had left Nuala at the bus-stop, he had fully intended to go home, take a shower (or a bath, since there wasn't a shower in his flat), change from his sweaty jeans and grandfather shirt to a clean pair of jeans and grandfather shirt, and go, dutifully, to Melissa's party. It was not one of his habits to break appointments of any kind: indeed, it was alien to his nature to do so. And anyway there was no good reason not to turn up at the party, which promised to be good fun. He knew and liked Melissa; he liked the way she looked and the way she spoke, and he liked the reassuring fact of her Americanness, with which he felt more at home than the characteristics of the Irish. And he appreciated the comforts of her lifestyle.

While he was walking from Ranelagh to Rathmines, in the cold dark evening in which the fresh smell of frost and the sourish smell of old leaves mingled, he whistled to himself, and allowed images of the horses, the fields he had ridden through, and various girls' faces, especially Vogue's, to pass through his mind in a leisurely disordered sequence. He was, in spite of the disapproving looks given him by Nuala, in good form. He had found the ride and the excursion in general very enjoyable, being, as Nuala knew, very fond of all natural things: in a way the outing to Enniskerry had come closer to fulfilling some of his expectations of Ireland than had most of the experiences he had had here so far, and he felt what he described as 'relaxed', a concept which was more important in Denmark than in Dublin. Although he did not think of Melissa's party while he walked, or devote any forethought to what he might wear, in sharp contrast to Nuala, who had been thinking for nothing else since she'd left Enniskerry, unconsciously he was preparing for the evening ahead: when he passed by the large newsagent's on the corner of Rathmines Road, he lingered for a moment looking at bunches of hothouse flowers which were displayed on a stand outside. He did not buy one for his hostess only because he didn't like the colours: lurid yellow, crimson and white, mixed together.

His change of heart came about while he was in the bath. The bathroom, which he shared with several other tenants, was functional rather than decorative, which is not to say that it functioned efficiently. On the contrary: its enormous geyser burned with the ferocity of hellfire, but sent forth the faintest trickle of boiling water. After twenty minutes the deep iron bath was less than a quarter full, and the room was saturated with dense steam. Through the haze, a sign painted in alarming red letters on the side of the geyser warned: 'Always have a window and door open while using the bath!' Irish tenants naturally ignored this, being accustomed to risking life and limb in the course of many of their daily activities. But Erik took the notice seriously, and so bathtime was a hurried, uncomfortable experience for him. He remembered, for a moment, looking over his shoulder to make sure no one was coming in, his mother's bathroom in Charlottenlund: its deep pink washable carpet, soft as mink on the feet, the rosy glow of its walls, the luxurious comfort of the sunken tub, and the lovely warmth of the room itself. In Charlottenlund, he had taken baths for the sheer luxury of it—showers were more commonplace, a part of the daily ablutions. Here there was no shower and one bathed only when strictly necessary, and often not even then, since it required an exceptional courage or an unusually pressing need to force one to face that bathroom.

Nuala was like the bathroom.

The thought came to him out of the blue, as he was wrapping himself in his thick, fluffy, dark-yellow towel and going back across the hall to his room. Yes. At first she had been consoling and warm, like the first gush of steam, like the first minute in the four inches of water. He had looked up to her as a wise, kind, gentle woman, one whom he considered to be older than himself, although in reality she was two years his junior. Initially, he had to admit, she had even reminded him a little of his mother, a woman given to occasional mood-swings, but essentially reliable, essentially always on his side. Over the past months, however, Nuala had changed dramatically. No longer the calm, thoughtful, almost calculating person he had admired and leant upon, she seemed to have gradually lost control of herself. She was full of resentments and petty jealousies; she nagged and questioned; she was clinging to him instead of letting him depend on her. Whereas she had been good for him to begin with, she was now, basically, bad for him, as he put it himself. He had never looked forward to his meetings with her all that much: she had been too patronising to begin with, and he had always had reservations about their 'love affair', which he had entered into from a sense of obligation more than from any natural desire for Nuala. For heaven's sake, she was not even all that pretty! But now he was often in dread of an encounter with her, and he particularly disliked being accompanied by her to parties thrown by his Trinity friends. She was becoming more and more of an irritation, a thorn in his side.

'I will not go!' he said to himself, in Danish, as he rubbed himself dry. And he laughed gently. 'I just won't go!' He pulled on fresh jeans and a new blue sweatshirt, recently sent to him by his mother (all his clothes were blue). Then he made himself an open sandwich, with some of the tasteless Irish bread and chunks of salty cheese and put on a Bob Dylan LP. He had no further plans now; the evening stretched emptily ahead of him. But he felt most relaxed, almost light-headed, because of the decision he had just taken. He would no doubt see Nuala again. No doubt their relationship would continue. But he had cut a cord. No longer was he bound to her by a sense of tradition or obligation. There was no law forcing him to spend tonight, or any other night, in her company, as she had somehow implied there was, especially during the past few months.

He made himself a second sandwich and wished he had a glass of lager to have along with it.

He had been in Ireland for two years now, and in a year hoped to finish his doctoral thesis and move home to Denmark or on to wherever he might get a job. His initial disappointment in Dublin had given way to a quiet tolerance— under Nuala's tutelage—and there were aspects of the place which he had come to appreciate. In particular he had enjoyed his journeys to Galway and Donegal, where he had spent a good portion of his holidays, somewhat to his mother's dismay, although he had spent the previous summer in Copenhagen. The 'nature', as he called it, was truly wonderful, and he had enjoyed meeting some of the old countrymen in the funny little pubs of the west, even though often the conversations did not amount to much in the final analysis. He was an admirer of Synge, and so his sojourn on the Aran Islands had meant a great deal to him, although there was disappointment there again, since so much had clearly changed for the worse since Synge had made his visits at the end of the nineteenth century. Not only did the women not wear red skirts or the men moccasins but the people were not at all as friendly and warm as Synge had described them and they could certainly no longer be considered as the most noble, self-contained, active human beings on God's earth. Neither were they as beautiful as Synge had made them out to be, especially not the women, whom Erik thought rather ugly. Still, the landscape itself had made up for much. And he also liked the traditional music, which he had plenty of opportunity to hear in the height of the tourist season, as it was while he was on the islands.

The Trinity life was also very amusing, in its way, although it did not differ markedly from student life in Copenhagen except in its acute physical discomforts. Once he had come to terms with the old-fashioned, dogmatic teaching style, the lack of a holistic approach to any topic, the complete contempt for all modernistic analytical methods—all of which they thought of as their high scholastic standards—he had learned to tolerate, if not actually like the place. Sometimes he even found himself coming round to the Irish way of thinking about scholarship. More and more often, recently, he had begun to doubt the tenets of structuralism, neo-structuralism and deconstruction, and wonder if old-fashioned postivitistic criticism were not, after all, the best. But of course it was an impossible solution, because it was a dead end. Unless you used the newest approaches all the time, there would be nothing left to study in Old English literature. Everything had been examined to within an inch of its life ten thousand times already. Your only hope was the latest theory.

And Erik had high hopes. He had invested time and, more significantly, money, in his education, unlike Nuala, who had never spent a penny on hers. Fees at Irish universities were high if you happened to be a foreigner, or indeed if you happened to be Irish and economically situated at a comfortable distance from the breadline where the Byrnes and their likes survived. Nuala, one of the tiny minority of working class Irish people to take what was on offer educationally, did not place an economic value on her achievements, such as they were. It had been handed to her on a plate and now she was willing to toss it all away. She was willing to give up. Oh well, she was a girl anyway; they never really make it acad-

emically. Haven't got what it takes. But he had.
And he would not give in.

He hoped very much to find employment in
Denmark. One benefit of the Irish experience
was that it had taught him to appreciate his
own country. In truth, he had not done so while
he actually lived there, considering it too
bureaucratic, too materialistic, too unimagin-
ative. All the usual things, what everyone
thinks about Scandinavian countries in general.
And of course it was all of these things. But,
while it was theoretically a relief not to have a
'personal number', and to know that the
revenue commissioners did not have a
computer filled with all relevant information
on one's lifestyle, while it was nice, in a
sentimental, odd way to live among people
who went to church on Sunday, in reality the
disadvantages of Irish life were much more
pressing and apparent. Church on Sunday, for
instance, while touching as an idea, had turned
out to be very boring indeed in practice. Erik
had gone once, to eleven o'clock Mass in
Rathmines. He had stood—with Nuala,
needless to add—at the back of an enormous,
over-decorated, positively ugly building, which
had been crammed with thousands of
shuffling, coughing, crying people. The priest
and his activities had been invisible. Over the
loudspeaker system, he had heard his voice
intoning the immortal words in a deep Cork
accent, which had been faintly amusing. But

the words themselves lacked interest. The whole experience had been a flop, as far as he was concerned. Like Mass, Ireland itself was old-fashioned and charming and moving, from a distant perspective. But once you experienced it at first hand, you found its details drab and its atmosphere dull. The price you had to pay for the lack of materialism was pathetic inefficiency: buses that did not run on time, tradesmen who did not come even on the day promised, let alone the hour, laws that were enacted but never put into practice, houses that were draughty and unheated. Materialists were more careful about such matters. Danes were anyway. Of late he had even begun to wonder if the Irish was lacking in materialism. Sometimes they seemed more materialistic than the Danes, more materialistic than anyone. They were certainly obsessed with money, and the lack of it, and they talked about it much more often and more vulgarly than any Dane would. There was a sort of brutality in the society, he sensed now, a sort of cruelty, born, perhaps, of the bad economy and the hopelessness. The tinkers begging on the streets of Dublin depressed him. Children with blue noses and ragged clothes drawing with coloured chalk on the pavement, for money, while the non-materialistic Irish dashed past, eyes carefully averted. Mothers with babies wrapped in their coats, sitting in the frost or rain on O'Connell Bridge, while the east wind whipped up the Liffey. It wasn't easy to live with them. Or with the easy acceptance of crime, theft and so on, and what went with that: the acceptance that some sizeable sections of the population were so deprived that they would of necessity turn to crime as an alternative to being completely downtrodden. The rawness of Dublin...the iciness of the bathroom...always bathing with windows and door open...Nuala's nagging, her constant anxieties about the future. They were all of a piece. He was looking forward to getting back to where people lived for the moment, fulfilled themselves, to where there were no beggars and everyone had a warm home and a hot bath whenever they felt like it, everyone from the latest immigrants from Turkey to the long-established residents of Charlottenlund, Copenhagen's second most salubrious suburb.

And he needed to be closer to his mother.

Erik's mother had been divorced almost as long as he could remember. He had been her only child, and under the circumstances they were very close. For years, always, really, they had been friends rather than mother and son. Kirsten was only twenty years older than he was, and had been a student during the first six years of his childhood. Now she was a successful doctor. She had been used to working so hard, however, as a single mother, that she had not a great circle of friends, and had grown rather dependent on Erik for company. Indeed, this very dependency had prompted him to apply for the Irish scholarship in the first place: he had felt that it would be good for Kirsten to learn to stand on her own feet and also he had found the dependency something of a burden. Where would it end? Now, however, at a comfortable distance, he was in a more considerate frame of mind. He would not live with his mother again. That had been his mistake. He would take an apartment in another part of the city, possibly on Amager, the smaller island, on which the university now had most of its premises and which was rather trendy in a shabby urban way. But he would be able to visit his mother regularly. They could be in touch without living in one another's ears. It was a desirable solution.

The Dylan record played itself out. Erik stayed on the rug in front of the electric fire for five more minutes. Then he telephoned Binjy, a friend in Trinity,who, miraculously, was in. They arranged to meet in O'Neill's of Suffolk Street at nine o' clock.

Binjy was waiting for him when he entered the pub at nine o'clock on the dot. Erik forged a path through the thick crowd, like some arboreal animal breaking through undergrowth in a forest, and finally hailed him in his characteristic, low-key style. Binjy, like Melissa an American but from the middle-west, from

Oklahoma, was not low-key at all. He grabbed Erik's hand and shook it very heartily, up and down, up and down several times, as if he had not seen him in a long time. Or as if he were welcoming him to his home for the first time.

And in a sense he was doing this. O'Neill's was his home, as near as you could get, in Dublin. He spent almost every evening and quite a large portion of his days as well on its convivial premises, chatting and joking with a varied, often changing, selection of friends and acquaintances from college and elsewhere. He could not have been termed the centre of any sort of social group, since there was not a group as such, but rather a kaleidoscope of changing, overlapping, different individuals, some of whom formed their own small groups, but most of whom did not, and had simply happened to become friendly with Binjy, who was a very friendly person. He held court: perhaps this is how one should put it. Although he was too modest and easygoing to play the role of king, that is what he was. King of the what?

Binjy had never been an especially close friend of Erik's, who did not have any close friends. (Neither did Binjy). He was not serious enough to attract him much as a friend, but Binjy's rakish ways appealed strongly to the side of his character which admired JP Dunleavy, not to speak of Jack Kerouac, and other beatnik writers, the sixties group.

Freedom of a kind was what Binjy was after, and life in the raw and a good time. A little of that would be no bad thing, it seemed to Erik now. He was ready for it. For too long he had submitted to mother, to Nuala, to rules and obligations.

He bought a pint for himself and for Binjy, and then sat down beside him. After the initial exchange of greetings, the slapping on the back and joking, there was not much to say. Erik was so habitually silent that it was very difficult for him to make small talk at any level; he had simply never learned how to do it. Banter was beyond him and although Binjy was extremely proficient in all the more superficial conversational arts he could not keep up the stream of witticism completely unaided. After a lengthy silence, of more than five minutes, during which the hum of conversation around them rose to a pitch which Erik found deafening, Binjy said, 'You all right, old man? Your canary ain't gone and died, has it?'

'No,' said Erik, laughing. 'I'm fine. I'm just not used to enjoying myself, that's all.'

'You'll soon change all that if you set your mind to it, boy! Ain't nothing easier than having a good time. Ain't nothing more important neither.'

'You're right. Did you always know that?'

'Shucks...I guess you could say I did, I guess I was born with that know-how, you know? Does a kid enjoy himself, though? I can't say for sure. But we can, at our age, that's for sure.'

'We are in our prime.'

'Yeah, we're in our prime. We've got to sow our wild oats right now, while we've still got the chance. The time is right and the place is here.'

'You think that is important?'

'Damned sure it's important, man!'

'Yes. I feel that instinctively at the moment. But I am not sure why.'

'It's a basis for a happy life, that's why. '

'But you are happy now too? The good time, as you call it, makes you happy?'

'Sure thing.'

Binjy was becoming embarrassed. A faint flush spread across his heavy farm-boy features, and his smile, almost a permanent feature, took on a fixed, taut aspect. He had been aware that he possessed a philosophy justifying, or inspiring, his present mode of life. He was not having fun for the sheer heck of it, but because he firmly believed that it was his duty to have fun, as he put it, at this time and in this place. But it was a bit heavyhanded to have to explain it all to someone else. It took some of the good out of it. It occurred to him that Erik was casing the joint, as it were, before renting a room in it himself. And he also knew, as anyone would, that it could not work on such a contrived basis. You could not step out of your shell one fine morning and say: 'Now I'm going to sow my wild oats.' Erik was a weirdo, no mistake.

'Hey, Jacinta!' Binjy spotted a friend in the crowd. A damsel to the rescue! His broad smile expanded in relief.

A small girl dressed all in black, and wearing a big black hat on her red hair, made her way towards them. Erik observed her with some annoyance. He had wanted to have a longer, more serious talk with Binjy, about having fun and the necessity thereof. Trust some girl to come along and spoil it.

Jacinta arrived at the table and Binjy stood up and kissed her, first on the cheeks and then on the mouth. They exchanged effusive and exaggerated greetings. Finally Binjy introduced Jacinta to Erik.

'Are you in Trinity?' Erik asked. Usually this was the first question he asked everyone, no matter what their age or appearance.

'Oh no, not yet,' Jacinta answered with a moue. 'I'm still at school. Rathdown.'

'Get down?'

'I go to a school called Rathdown School. Its near Dun Laoghaire. I'm doing the Leaving next year, and then I hope to go to Trinity.'

'Good,' said Erik. 'I hope you do go to Trinity. It's a fun place to be.'

'Yes I know. I'm so grateful to Binjy for initiating me. I feel I'm a student already!'

'Jacinta's a great horsewoman.' Binjy changed the subject. 'That ought to interest you, old man. You're into horses too, aren't you? Erik's a great horseman,' he said, turning to Jacinta suddenly.

'Oh...' Erik felt too tired all of a sudden to disclaim the praise. What if Jacinta thought he was a great horseman? Did it matter what she thought?

Binjy took Jacinta and placed her on his lap, as if she were a doll. She sat there quite unconcernedly and drank her drink, which seemed to be an orange juice. Then she lit a cigarette and smoked it through a holder which was about five inches long. She puffed rings into the air, where they very quickly merged with the thick cloud of smoke with which the pub was filled. Erik watched, amused at this precocious schoolgirl. How silly she was in her antics and her attempts to be cool and grown-up. He was so absorbed in looking at her that he did not notice the approach of her best friend.

'Vogue!' shouted Jacinta at the top of her lungs. 'You're dead late, you silly coot! Where on earth have you been?'

'Sorreee!' hooted Vogue. Erik turned to look but he already knew.

'Hi!' he said somewhat tersely. 'We meet again.'

'Hello!' Vogue smiled very sweetly and turned her eyes modestly towards the floor, in the eternal gesture of submission. 'What a surprise to meet you here.'

'Life is full of surprises,' said Erik, 'not all of

them as pleasant as this one.'

His first attempt at gallantry. Ever. It worked, of course. In no time at all, Vogue was sitting on his knee, drinking lemonade and, mercifully, not smoking anything at all.

CHAPTER SIX

When Nuala asked Erik why he had not come to the party, he said he had been so tired after riding that he had fallen asleep and not woken up until almost two o'clock in the morning, by which time it was too late to do anything, even telephone her. It was the first time he had ever lied to her, and one of the first—though not the first—times he had ever lied at all. He had beginner's luck and she believed him, although she was encouraged in this attitude as much by her own sense of guilt, at having enjoyed the party, as by her faith in his truthfulness: Nuala believed that a Dane was unlikely to be dishonest, although she would not have trusted an Irishman farther than she could throw him.

Besides, she was not ready for the consequences of disbelief.

She was fully aware that their relationship was changing. For many months Erik had been independent of her as a nurse and psychiatric adviser. He could function very capably on his own. She felt a natural slight regret at this fact in itself, as every nurse, every teacher, ever parent who has grown fond of his charge must do when the job is done satisfactorily and the patient, pupil or child is discharged from their care. At first she had not worried about any danger to the 'relationship': she was blinded, perhaps by her the strength of her attachment, to any possible fragility in Erik's feelings for her. Besides, she had been very busy, completing her MA thesis, which she had worked on with enthusiasm, becoming feverishly active during its final stages. Erik had appeared to be equally engrossed in his studies and it had not occurred to her than his heart could have had the opportunity to wander away from her.

For a while, however, she had been aware of a change. It dated from about the time she had made her decision about the job in the Civil Service. In so doing she had been carrying out Erik's wish, and one might have assumed that he would have been grateful and appreciative of her heroic self-sacrifice. The contrary was true. Almost as soon as she had committed herself to taking the job, Erik had begun to pull away from her. It was as if, because she was having bad luck occupationally, bad luck insisted on dogging her in every other aspect of her life as well—and very quickly Erik forgot entirely why Nuala had taken the job in the first place. Nuala began to forget that herself. In the day-to day-routine, one could not recall everything; one could not recall the day of freedom, the time of choice. To do so, in fact, would have been intolerable. It is not easy to forgive oneself for being stupid, no matter how good the reason for it at the time.

From the time of the party, Erik became more and more irritable, more intolerant of Nuala's faults. He nagged and complained: she was too timid, she was too aggressive, she was too unambitious, she was too ambitious, she was overactive, she was nervous. Her clothes were awful. She was getting fat. In short, he began to hate her.

'Our sex life is not satisfactory,' he told her one evening, after they had been making love— although at this point that was not the appropriate term—in his flat.

'Isn't it?' Nuala had taken to responding to most of these remarks either with silence or with a rhetorical question. In this case, she agreed with him. Their sex life was not satisfactory. Their love life was not satisfactory. Nothing in their life was satisfactory. But she was reluctant to admit any of this, least of all to Erik.

'No. It is not. And it never has been.'

Erik was sitting up in bed. He was naked, but he wore his small gold reading glasses far down on his nose. His expression was grimly censorious. Nuala felt that she was being examined by a particularly harsh and demanding schoolmaster. She noticed anew how ugly the room was, with its cheap furniture and hard grey light. Could anyone have a satisfactory sex life in such surroundings? She began to pull on her pants.

'I suppose not.'

They had had problems. Nuala when she met Erik was a virgin, belonging as she did to the generation of Irish people who never went the whole way, although they came close. Erik had had to persuade her to do it his way, the genuine way, the Scandinavian way. All or nothing. First they had used condoms, of which he had possessed an endless supply, thoughtfully taken with him from home. They had not been a success. Nuala, terrified of becoming pregnant, did not trust the flimsy sausage balloons which Erik referred to as 'rubbers' and reacted to his advances with physical asperity. The sexual experience, which she had enjoyed before it became so serious, was transformed to a difficult acrobatic exercise, unpleasurable at best, painful most of the time. Blaming the technology rather than her, Erik had persuaded her to go to a family planning centre and get the pill. He was convinced that, once they could make love 'naturally', all would be well. Nuala had been only too willing.

The trip to the clandestine clinic, which was situated on a small seedy residential street behind Camden Street, she had found thrilling: the sense of subterfuge, of crime, of brave libertinism were considerably more invigorating than tussling with Erik on a spongy mattress. She enjoyed sneaking down the steps to the basement where the clinic was so aptly situated, listening to the bright cheerful receptionist and doctor dispensing advice in their glamorous English accents— English accents were *de rigueur*. And the wonderful questions they asked: Are you married? Are you engaged? How often do you have sex? And the brave brilliant answers. No. No. Well...

The pill came in slender green-and-white packets and looked friendly and harmless. Nuala swallowed their contents faithfully, never missing a day, and when a month had passed she had gained half a stone, suffered from bouts of morning sickness and was ready to have sex without rubber. Erik tried to be patient and kind; he was in a classic 'Darling, I'll try not to be rough with you!' mood when they did it the first time. But Nuala did not believe in the Pill either: she could not believe that such a simple precaution would really work. Or so she rationalised the matter, for she continued apprehensive and, as Erik was beginning to put it to himself, frigid. He hadn't read David Lodge, he didn't know much about the bodies of young women. He didn't know about Vaseline. Neither did Nuala. For both of them the main source of information on sexuality had been the novels of DH Lawrence. Emotionally, Nuala had everything in common with Lady Chatterley. But her body was twenty years younger than that character's, apart from not being the creation of a male author's imagination, and to her horror her first experiences of the sexual act were much less than earth-shattering. She pretended, however, to enjoy it, in order to placate Erik, and had even gone the whole hog and feigned orgasm, which she had regularly had before they started having proper sex. Apparently she hadn't pretended hard enough. He'd noticed that she was wincing most of the time.

Fully dressed, in jeans and chunky sweater, she sat on the edge of the bed. Erik was lying down, reading a comic: he harboured a strange childish interest in Disney cartoons and kept a supply of suitable magazines, sent from Denmark, in the flat.

'I'm going to go home now,' she said in what she hoped was a suitably sad but firm tone.

'Goodbye.'

He looked up briefly from Mickey Mouse and grinned faintly and sardonically at her. She took her coat and left.

It was a freezing cold night, and her footsteps rang out against the icy pavement. The silver railings dividing the path from the long dark gardens gleamed and the street lamps glowed like lighted pumpkins, just that same lurid orange colour. She sucked in the frosty air. Usually this kind of night, a fine winter's night, filled her with the joys of living, injected her with energy. Normally in these circumstances her footsteps would lighten and she would fly along, run or walk for miles, needing to burn up excess vitality.

Tonight she moved heavily homeward.

It was all so awful.

Erik was pulling away from her, trying desperately to escape. And the harder he pulled the harder she pulled. It was a tug of war, and she was the one who was down now and needed help. Help. Help. She wanted him to marry her.

Marry. Marry. Once she said that word to herself, much became clear.

She was twenty-two, in 1975. In San Francisco, the hippies were going out and the yuppies were already toilet-trained. In Denmark, marriage had been all but replaced by the paperless marriage or living in sin. In Dublin, the pressure was on.

All around her, people were marrying as if a Third World War were on the doorstep. All the students she had known as an undergraduate were buying engagement rings, saving for a mortgage, having their hair styled into matronly coiffures. All the MAs had gone to America, where everyone marries eventually. All the civil servants were either married already—in the case of men—or talking about it, in the case of women: since the 'Marriage Bar' had been lifted two years ago they could afford to do so without putting their jobs in jeopardy, though many still saw marriage as an escape from the demands or tedium of the job.

In the Civil Service, there were three kinds of women: women who were hoping to get engaged, women who were already engaged, and women who had given up. (In addition there was a handful of widows, but Nuala had not come across them since there were none in her department. She had not come across any married women either).

The members of the third category were, if They were elderly, feared and somewhat despised by the first group, who whispered among themselves in paroxyms of prejudice. They hated men, because they'd been ditched by one thirty years before. They hated girls, especially if they were attractive. They were cross bosses, inefficient workers. They drank, they gambled, they were going mad.

These women were not, of course, avoided by everyone, only by girls in category number one, girls who were not engaged but had hopes. Girls like Nuala. The cause of the prohibition was fear of contamination. It was a delicate situation. Conditioned since birth to desire marriage above all else (as Victorian girls in England and America are said to have desired it), they realised that their wish, their deep-seated long-lived ambition, was under siege from all sorts of sources. Women's lib, for instance. The perceived antipathy of middle-class Irishmen to marriage, for another. The influence of spinsters, for a third. Such people might, somehow, by persuasion or example, discourage one. They would suggest alternatives, somehow, and some atavistic intelligence warned Nuala that unless she really wanted to get married she would not marry. The opportunities would slip past her, the men would escape, as received wisdom suggested they all wanted to. Only the most beautiful had any hope of ensnaring a man without effort, although it was surprising how many truly beautiful women in Dublin remained unwed anyway. Dublin men required even more than perfect beauty; what, one could not know. For those who were not perfect lovelies, wit and will and guile and skill would be essential.

In Nuala's office, there was one engaged girl—Pauline. She was a stereotypical engaged girl: smart and slender and carefully groomed. She wore fluffy angora sweaters and slim-fitting skirts; pink and black was a favourite colour combination with her, or turquoise and black, and her shoes were always high-heeled black pumps which showed off her trim legs to great advantage. A lot of her time at the office was spent in the loo, touching up her make-up or back-brushing her silvery hair.

Tommy and Sean teased her constantly. (The concept of sexual harrassment had not yet been hatched, fortunately for the entertainment standards of the office.)

'And how is the lovely Pauline Coffey this

morning?' Tommy would ask as she drifted in, on the dot of nine fifteen. 'Get your beauty sleep, Pauline? Need to store up energy, you know, for the honeymoon."

'Need you ask?' Sean would attempt to mimic Pauline's voice, and produced a ridiculous high falsetto. 'I look beautiful, don't I? It's because I use Oil of Ulay. Gentle enough for a baby's skin. I'm going to use it on my baby's bum when I get one. The acid test!'

At this point, Pauline would throw something at Sean: a packet of envelopes, or a bundle of memos, anything she happened to have on her inordinately neat desk. Even the neatness seemed to be part of it, part of the game, what one had to be to deserve marriage. The most feminine little girls were always the neatest.

Another person who was going to be married was Nuala's friend, Jean, a girl she had known since her schooldays. She had announced her engagement at midsummer, on her birthday, but she had not yet announced the date of the wedding.

'Well, we're dying to get married, really dying to. I mean we really do love one another very much, and I must say I think we're very well matched. I think we belong together; do you know what I mean? I can't imagine, I just can't imagine marrying anyone else, I really just can't imagine it, and I don't think Cyril could either. I shouldn't speak for him, I really don't know but I don't think so.'

She paused, briefly for breath. Nuala nodded, encouragingly. She could not find anything to say. Jean's effusiveness, which she admired for its energy, often subdued her to the point of speechlessness.

'But we can't get married until we've got a house, we just can't. We'd love to, we'd really love to, but we can't because it would be so foolish. I mean only two real fools would get married with nowhere to live. Don't you agree?'

'Oh yes,' said Nuala, who did not agree at all.

'Sometimes, only sometimes, I'm tempted. I really am. I'm tempted to say, "Hang it all!" and go into a flat. But it's only temporary, I wouldn't do it because I know it's a recipe for disaster, it really is.'

Why? wondered Nuala, as she sat silent, and observed Jean's round head, circled with neat blond curls, bobbing up and down, from side to side, as if she were a puppet and it were on a string.

'Oh, that reminds me!' Jean widened her eyes and leaned across the table, confidentially. 'We got an invitation to Elinor's wedding. Remember Elinor?'

'Yes.'

'Well, Elinor is getting married to Michael. Remember Michael?'

'Yes.'

'He's very nice. They're both very nice, although sometimes I've found Elinor very unfriendly. The last time I met her on the street she passed me by without talking! I was most surprised to receive the invitation, most surprised! She's always been fond of Cyril, that's probably why we got it; it's not because of me! She doesn't like me; I really don't know why. I mean I don't think I'm such an awful person really!'

'Oh no!'

'But...' She lowered her voice. 'It's very sad about the wedding, it's very sad. I mean, what are they going to do? Where are they going to go?'

Nuala shrugged. Where was anyone going to go?

'They haven't got a house, they haven't got a deposit for a mortgage. She doesn't even have a job! It's depressing to even think about it! I'd rather her than me!'

'Yes.'

How can this relationship continue, Nuala asked herself, if all she was ever allowed to say was 'yes'? It was really unbelievable, it was unbelievable really, really it was unbelievable ...perhaps she should try repeating everything three times, and become 'a talker' too. Perhaps then Jean would be her friend and not just someone she met for lunch. Perhaps if she talked more she would have more women friends. Perhaps perhaps perhaps.

Unexpectedly and uncharacteristically, Jean abruptly changed the subject. 'Will you look around the shops with me after lunch? I've got nothing to wear, not a stitch. I really have to get something.'

'Love to,' said Nuala, truthfully. She looked around the shops every lunchtime. It was a habit, possibly becoming an addiction. Shopaholism. 'Had you anything in mind?'

'Oh well, something nice but something practical, you know, that I can use afterwards. I don't want to get something that I can never wear again. I just can't afford that; it's a luxury I just can't afford. Something nice, and warm, and practical. I mean it's going to be December, what a time for a wedding!'

'Yes. Poor Elinor. What will she wear, I wonder?'

'God, as long as it's big enough it doesn't matter.' Jean grimaced, for just long enough to let her message sink in. Then she smiled very sweetly. 'Let's look in Mirror Mirror first, will we?'

'Yes, let's,' said Nuala flatly.

Perhaps she didn't want Jean as a friend anyway. But she needed woman friends.

She'd had best friends at school. A girl called Barbara, with long tawny fair hair, had sat beside her right through Primary. They had shared an antipathy to needlework which had kept them together for so long: neither of them could sew at all, in a school where sewing was taken very seriously. Also they lived not too far from one another, and walked home from school together every afternoon, Nuala to Exeter Place and Barbara to her flat in an old, ramshackle house on the Rathmines Road. Because of this address, because she lived in a flat and not in a house, Mollie had disapproved of her and had made many attempts to break up the friendship. These had ultimately failed. But they did affect Nuala's attitude: she held Barbara in affectionate contempt; she resented Mollie's criticisms of her which mainly concerned Barbara's hair: there were nits in it, Mollie said. She had seen them there herself. It was not until many years later than Nuala realise that Mollie was obsessed with nits. And with worms. She saw traces of them everywhere, in every head and every bottom. It is surprising, however, how the accusation of lousiness can diminish a person's status. Barbara never had any, in Nuala's eyes. She merely tolerated her. Perhaps this had affected her attitude to women friends in general? They never quite came up to the mark, the mark which had been set by Mollie. They were all infected with some sort of symbolic nits. Which boys did not have.

When she went to secondary school, a different one from Barbara's, she made friends with a tall, thin aristocratic-looking girl called Mary Rose. Mary Rose Tynan. In this relationship, the inferior partner had been

Nuala. Socially inferior, that is. Mary Rose's father had been a schoolteacher and the Tynans lived in a new semi-detached house in Dundrum and were the essence of respectability. Mollie had loved Mary Rose and was constantly inviting her around for tea. But these occasions had been torture for Nuala. She watched Mary Rose observing everything: the old house, the old furniture, the bathroom tacked on to the kitchen. The shrieking carpet on the hall. The problem with Mary Rose was more serious than the problem with Barbara, Nuala knew. Mary Rose did not come down to the mark, the real mark set by brass tacks. In the end she ditched Nuala and made friends with Monica Walshe from Templeogue. Nuala had known it would have to come to that. She'd waited for it.

Erik thought she should have more friends.

It was another one of his hobby-horses, part of his overall critique.

'We should have more friends…see more people. Young people like us should get a bit of fun out of life.'

Was this the former would-be suicide, the Christ figure, the poet talking? Nuala tried to pinpoint the style: she'd heard it before somewhere.

'I suppose you're right,' she agreed half-heartedly. 'But we do meet people and so on; we aren't all that claustrophobic.'

'I don't mean that we should meet people

together, as a couple. I believe we should have more friends as separate individuals. I should have more, and...' his voice took on a slow meaningful pace, 'you should have more.'

Nuala struggled to defend herself but it wasn't easy. On the one hand, she was sure that Erik was out to get her now. Nothing she did or was could possibly have his approval. On the other hand she found herself in agreement with a lot of his fault-finding: she was an inadequate person. Not the woman he had believed her to be, last year or the year before, but a weakling. The worst fault now was loving him and wanting to be with him. What had been gloriously right a year ago was now a mark of failure.

'I have friends!' Her voice became petulent. 'There's Jean. And Brenda. And...'

There was no one else. Nuala had long ago dropped most of her women friends in favour of Erik. She hadn't needed anybody else while she had him. They had been such good friends! But he had forgotten all that.

'Jean and Brenda. I know. One is mad and one is a stodgy married lady. It's important for you to have friends who are real companions to you. Women you can talk to, who share some of your interests.'

'I'm sure you're right. I'd like to have friends like that...but I'm not sure that I can find them.'

'You can find them if you try.'

CHAPTER SEVEN

Earlier in the year Erik had invited Nuala to
spend Christmas with him and his mother in
Copenhagen. She had bought her ticket as soon
as the invitation had been issued, in order, she
explained, to avail of the cheaper fares
available to those who booked in advance, and
also, as she did not explain but as Erik
understood, to ensure that he could not change
his mind. Although relations between them
were almost as chilly as the northern winter
Erik was too honourable to cancel the trip, and
Nuala, while getting increasingly wearied by
the morbidity of it all, was too desperate to pull
out of her own accord.

Erik flew home a week earlier than Nuala:
she had so few holidays, or 'leave' as it was
somewhat quaintly described in Civil Service
jargon, that she waited until the day before
Christmas Eve to make the journey.

She saw Erik off at the airport. 'Saw off' is
the appropriate term: wet-eyed and heavy-
hearted, she gazed at him walking though the
barrier that led to the departure tunnel,
watched as he turned and waved, sternly, when
he'd got through, then watched his tall,

sheepskin-covered back move along the tunnel towards oblivion. At that point, the moving down the tunnel point, she had felt that she might do something desperate and dramatic: faint, for instance, or have a heart attack; her sense of loss was so strong that it demanded some violent expression. She realised, however, that any display of emotion would be anathema to Erik, so she bit her lip and controlled herself until he eventually disappeared from her line of vision. Then, walking very slowly, like an invalid or an extremely old woman, she left the terminal and waited for a bus back to town. The bus-stop was just outside the exit from the terminal in a grey concrete porch. The view was of cars driving along the circular concrete road, cars parked in the vast car park, various grey concrete buildings: a view of glass and concrete and steel, a technology-scape. She felt like a machine herself, dull and colourless and turned off. But to her surprise this mood changed with great rapidity, and without her willing it to do so. While she was still at the bus-stop, in fact, as a thick fog is scattered by a sudden wind, she felt her spirits lift. There was a physically perceptible lightening of mood and she could sense a burden falling from her shoulders. By the time she had caught the bus and was in O'Connell Street, indulging her shopping addiction, she was as happy as a lark, a lark which has recently bathed in a cool refreshing pond and is now soaring higher than ever, with squeaky-clean feathers. In short and less romantic terms, she was pleased as punch that Erik was no longer around.

Freedom. Liberty. Equilibrium.

Nobody nagging.

Nobody staring censoriously at her over the rims of his spectacles.

Nobody wishing she did not exist.

Nobody at her.

And how did she use her freedom?

Making preparations for the reunion, how else? Buying presents for Erik and his mother, buying clothes for herself. Her arrangements in this regard were most elaborate. She viewed Erik's mother, Erik's friends, Erik's relatives, and the people of Denmark in general, as judges. They would be assessing her suitability as a mate for their compatriot, examining her in detail, particularly as far as appearance was concerned. She must pass muster. She must have the best of everything. New trousers, new jumpers, new coat, new boots. A new hairstyle. She went to 'The Witches Hut' on Nassau Street, at that time the most fashionable and expensive hairdressers in Dublin, and had her shoulder-length hair cut, permed and tinted. She emerged with a fluffy copper cap of butter curls. 'Takes years off you!' Tommy said when she came back to the office. 'You look about thirteen!' And he guffawed at Sean. So what if she looked a few years younger, or older, if that's what he really meant. It was sophisticated: she hardly recognised herself in the looking glass.

Mary helped her pack, rather surprisingly, since she did not as a rule behave in a chummy sisterly fashion. Nor was she often present at 6 Exeter Place. Her new boyfriend took up a great deal of her time, and usually she did not even sleep at home. Mollie and Dessie turned a blind eye to this slightly aberrant behaviour; they were too old to care any more what their daughters did. Nuala had hardly set eyes on Mary in two months. But the night before the departure for Denmark Mary materialised for dinner, and afterwards accompanied Nuala to their shared bedroom where she immediately began to examine the contents of her wardrobe.

'Lovely!' she said, stroking a burgundy velvet jacket. 'You're so lucky, having all these lovely clothes!'

Mary was dressed, as usual, in blue jeans and a yellow shetland jumper.

'You will, too, soon.' Nuala did not bother to refute the implication, although of course it annoyed her. 'Your thesis must be nearly finished by now, isn't it?'

'Oh that!' She tossed her head and then nodded it mournfully. 'It'll never be finished. I haven't done a thing with it since October.'

Nuala looked at her sharply. 'Why not?'

'I'm sure you know why not.'

Nuala had no idea. But she was anxious to

find out and in order to do so she knew she would have to preserve this mood of confidentiality. Unfortunately she did not really know how best to do so, or to elicit information. A minute's silence had no effect. Finally she risked, bluntly: 'It's because you're involved with someone, I suppose.'

It sounded pathetic. 'Involved with someone.' But she could not bring herself to use a less clumsy phrase.

'Yes, I'm involved with someone, of course. The ancient, classic, "Drop everything, you're involved with someone". Sure. That's it. Involved. For Christ's sake, I'm in love, not involved, inloved. Involved, infooled, in love.'

In for a penny, in for a pound, thought Nuala, faintly amused at Mary's anger. (But failing utterly to notice her attempt at Joycean language play. She was so steeped in courses in English Literature still that she took such things for granted.)

'Who is he?'

'I don't think it's anybody you know.'

Nuala set her mouth grimly. Bloody mean of her, to lead her on in this way and then fail to deliver. And typical. She folded a chiffon blouse, which billowed out in snowy wings at the shoulders and refused to be confined in a small flat space.

'It's John. John Smyth,' Mary said, suddenly.

John Smyth. Not an uncommon name. But Nuala blushed with embarrassment. There was only one John Smyth she could mean.

'You mean…?'

'Yes.'

John Smyth. Lecturer in Old Irish, Mary's thesis supervisor. Nice, but in an eccentric style. Attractive, also in an eccentric style. Attractive, that is, for a man aged at least fifty. (He'd always been eccentric, according to gossip: his entire reputation was founded on the rude things he had said to students during his nearly thirty years' employment in Fairfield).

'Well.' Nuala pushed the chiffon blouse into a corner of the suitcase and clamped it in with a pair of rolled up boots backed up by a fat hardback novel. 'That sounds interesting.'

What she thought was that it sounded revolting, and silly, and dangerous. And wasn't he married? Not that that would matter, with a person like him. Rude to students, rude to wives.

'Yes, it is interesting.' Mary's eyes brightened. She sat up straight and clasped her knees. 'We get on very well together. I know the whole thing must seem odd to people, but we do.'

'Well, at least you have plenty in common. Something to talk about.'

She didn't believe this either. What would they talk about anyway? The infixed pronoun? Stories from the *Táin*? As far as she'd noticed all Old Irish academics, or any other kind, in Fairfield talked about who was due to get promotion and why so-and-so was always going on lecture tours to America, while they themselves were too busy or too dedicated or too unlucky ever to go anywhere. Come to think about it, their conversation was not in any way more intellectual or interesting than the conversation of the Civil Service canteen, except that the men in college didn't discuss Sunday's match quite to the same extent.

'Oh yes.' Mary hopped up and examined a glittering lurex party dress critically. It was difficult to envisage a situation in which Nuala would wear this extravagant and flashy creation. It reminded Mary of prostitutes in a film she'd seen with John a few weeks earlier. What was it called? 'We do. We have a good relationship, at every level, I must say.'

Irma La Douce. It was. Nuala La Douce?

Good sex too, she means. Perhaps success comes with experience. Thought Nuala, without envy. Better bad sex, or none at all, with Erik, than multiple orgasms with John Smyth, in her opinion.

'That's good.' She offered this blandly. 'But, why have you stopped working on your thesis?'

'You know how it is!'

Nuala didn't. She and Erik had helped each other with their work. For the first year they had spent every day and evening sitting side by side in the library, studying and writing. It had been a wonderful year.

'You'll get back to it soon, I suppose?'

'Oh, yes, of course I will. I'm going to really get stuck into it after Christmas. It's my new year resolution. It'll be finished by June.'

Let's hope the fact that you're sleeping with the chief examiner doesn't prejudice your chances. And since when had Mary started using phrases like 'stuck into it'?

'That sounds sensible. You can do it. I know you can, if you try.'

How generous I am, thought Nuala, with advice and good counsel. It seemed to her that nobody, from Mary to her parents to her friends, had ever given her good advice. So short is human memory!

CHAPTER EIGHT

Erik came to Kastrup Airport to meet Nuala. He stood at the barrier in the Arrivals Hall and fixed his gaze on the door through which she would come. He'd had a traumatic week and was, for once, dying to see her.

He waited and waited. Then, after about two hundred passengers from Dublin had swung through the doors, she appeared. Yes, it was Nuala all right. But...What had she done to her hair? And those clothes! She was wearing a fur jacket, a patently fake fox-fur, a tight, calf-length black skirt, high heeled pumps and a large fur hat, a Cossack affair. It matched the jacket, and also the hair, which had changed colour since Erik had last seen it. As had her face, painted a pale brown, and her lips, dyed a brilliant red. What was this, some kind of extravagant and tasteless practical joke?

'Nuala!' His voice quavered, but she detected, mingling diffidently amidst the disapproval, a little surprise crotchet of genuine welcome. 'It's good to see you.'

But this was overwhelming. It's good to see her, Nuala, the bane of his life! God, what was wrong with the Danes, that they had lowered Erik's standards so terribly?

He pushed aside her trolley—laden with bags and a huge suitcase, as well as several plastic carryalls from the duty-free shop—and hugged her. She felt her body relax, instantly, totally, and so did he. Physically, certainly, they had missed one another. Their bodies, so used to being together, in bed and out of it, seemed to have sensitivities of their own, and were now behaving according to patterns which had little connection with the consciousness of at least one of owners, Nuala assumed.

'You look wonderful!'

This was Nuala, of Erik. He had, true to his initial impulse, bathed and shaved and had his hair trimmed. He had also discarded his Dublin clothes and rigged himself out in decent Danish casuals. What he wore was practically a uniform for all people under the age of forty in the country that winter: a huge green parka lined with green-white-and-black checked fur, thick corduroy pants, in dark blue, and a light-blue sweater. The rugged, casual look suited him and he looked much less like a suffering mendicant friar than he had in Dublin.

'You too!' said Erik, in a weak and unconvincing tone. But to squeeze that much out, to lie about a matter such as her appearance! That was the sort of thing silly drips might do, it was the sort of thing girls and mothers and aunties and grannies did. One did not expect it of the like of Erik.

'Thank you. I got my hair done,' she said unnecessarily. She patted the bit that was not covered by her hat. 'Do you like it?'

'It's very nice.' Erik squeezed her around the waist. 'Welcome to Copenhagen. I hope you have a wonderful time here.'

Here he overstepped the boundaries of decency, not to speak of credibility. 'I hope you have a wonderful time here!' It stank.

'How is your mother?'

Erik squirmed visibly. Nuala congratulated herself on having so quickly come to the nub of the problem.

'She's very well,' he said. 'Why don't we go now, and you'll meet her.'

Nuala was impressed by what she saw on the drive, and delighted with the house in Charlottenlund. Of respectable age—in Ireland Nuala would have said 'Victorian', but that didn't apply here—surrounded by a large garden generously planted with trees, it was spacious and beautiful. She admired the polished wooden floors, the rag rugs scattered gaily upon them like towels spread to dry on a golden beach, the innumerable lamps and candles, the stiff old furniture and the practical, suave modern stuff.

'I've never been in such a lovely house before!' She beamed at Erik and at Kirsten, when she had spent two minutes in the hall. 'It's so beautiful.'

They're rolling, of course. Why can't the men I like be poor, like me? But what the hell. It's fun. I can take some riches. The prince and half the kingdom. If I marry Erik I'll not only be married and triumphant and successful, I'll be rich as well. He's the genuine article, the prince of the kingdom of the eastern world.

'I will show you to your room.' Kirsten smiled at her. She was dubious, on account of the copper curls and the auburn furs, but perhaps Nuala was nicer than she looked. 'This way, please.'

'Oh, lovely!' Nuala looked with pleasure at the small neat chamber that had been assigned to her. It belonged to the part of the house that was decorated in a contemporary style: there was striped wallpaper, striped curtains and quilt to match, and various pieces of fitted furniture in natural wood. The floor was covered in hessian and the colour scheme in general was dark-blue and white. 'This looks really comfortable.'

Not quite Cinderella's wedding suite, but it'll do very nicely. Personally I prefer the modernist style. And this is the kind of room I wanted throughout my childhood, when I was sharing with Mary and even, at one stage before Dessie put up the partition, with Christopher. There was never enough room— or chintzy stuff or ribbons and bows in bedrooms in Exeter Place. They were furnished austerely with second-hand junk bought at the Rathmines Auction Rooms. Mollie, a brilliantly clean housekeeper, was not skilful in the creation of pretty feminine touches. She didn't have a feminine touch; it must be an attribute of the bourgeoisie. Oh well, better late than never.

'Yes. Well, when you are ready, you will join us for coffee?'

'Oh yes.'

Nuala was left on her own to unpack. She did this with surprising rapidity, considering how long it had taken her to pack in the first place, and she presented herself for coffee in the kitchen with great promptness.

Kirsten, Elsa and Erik were there, sitting round the table, waiting for the coffee machine to finish brewing. A stern looking woman whom Nuala had not seen before sat with them.

Kirsten stood up when Nuala entered. 'Nuala,' she said, more stiffly even than before. 'I'd like you to meet Elsa Groning. Elsa is my lover, and she lives here with us.'

'Pleased to meet you,' said Nuala, extending her hand mechanically. Elsa took it and shook it in her slender but very strong hand.

'Welcome to Denmark!' said Elsa. 'You have not been here before, I take it?

I must be the colour of a bloody lobster!

'Oh no, never,' mumbled Nuala. 'I'm very glad to have the opportunity.'

She glanced at Erik, who averted his eyes.

Kirsten was busy with the coffee machine. She poured four mugs of strongly smelling liquid and got a tin of biscuits from a cupboard on the wall.

'You must have some of these, Nuala,' she said. 'They are *peberkager*. I do not know the English...'

'Gingersnaps,' said Elsa, whose English was of a higher standard than Kirsten's, in consequence of her having spent six months in London as an au pair girl when she was twenty. And of being a competent kind of person. Her voice, even when speaking English, which she did with a very heavy accent, was thick with authority. You knew, hearing that tone, that Elsa believed she was always right, about every single thing.

'Ah. Gingersnaps. We make them every Christmas. They are very important to us in Denmark. '

'We cannot survive the season of goodwill without our gingersnaps!' Elsa laughed heartily. She had a deep-toned, sneering laugh: she was laughing at someone.

'Elsa made these actually,' nodded Kirsten, smiling. 'Here, take one or two.'

Nuala the Irish Girl, anxious to please (ATP), did. Her colour was still high but she could feel a return to normality. Oh well, travel broadens the mind. Chart it all up to experience. Never know when this bit will come in handy.

They all sipped and munched in silence. Elsa ate and drank delicately but with concentration: nourishment appeared to be a serious matter as far as she was concerned. Erik sulked but tucked away more bikkies than anyone else. Kirsten sat and sipped her coffee with the calm, ladylike indifference to food and drink which was characteristic of her. Even in that get-up you keep imagining her as someone in a simple little Chanel frock, Nuala thought. She's naturally elegant. She's naturally stylish. She's marvellous! No wonder Erik looks so handsome, with her as a mother. What can the da be like?

Her ponderings were rudely interrupted when, the coffee almost finished, Kirsten suddenly announced in a peremptory tone: 'We are very glad you are with us, Nuala, at this time. It is a very important time for us.'

'Christmas is important, isn't it?' Nuala, ATP, trained since babyhood to acquiese to every opinion, jumped in to agree wholeheartedly.'

'I do not mean Christmas.' Kirsten tossed her head with delicate scorn. 'I mean our wedding.'

'Yes?' Nuala looked at Erik, and at Elsa, and at Kirsten. She spilled some drops of coffee on her good black skirt.

'Elsa and I are getting married the day after tomorrow. We are so glad you can be with us.'

'Oh, you're getting married?' Nuala bought time, and crumbled what remained of her gingersnap (What a fuss about nothing! Those gingersnaps.) into her lap. This was an unconscious gesture, noticed by everyone except her. 'Well, that's wonderful. Congratulations.

115

I'm glad to be here, too.'

I wouldn't have missed it for the world. I do hope you'll be very happy. And have fine weather for the photographs, that's important, isn't it? You can ensure sunshine by placing a broken statue of the Child of Prague on the windowsill the night before. Maybe you should try that? I'd have brought one with me if I'd known.

'Good. I am pleased you feel so about it. Elsa and I are happy. For us it is a most important occasion, of course. We want to celebrate it with joy.'

'Oh, naturally,' agreed Nuala. Erik was washing a cup at the sink. The back of his neck was crimson, but perhaps that was due to the temperature in the kitchen: the heat was on full blast.

'We have it in the chapel at Humlebaek, a little village half way between this place and Helsingor.'

'Oh Elsinore! I'm dying to see Elsinore. We did *Hamlet* in school, for examinations but also on the stage. I played Rosencrantz. After reading it for three years and playing in it you really get to like a play!'

'It is not Elsinore; it is Humlebaek.There is a priest there who marries gays, that is why we choose it, no other reason. It will be at three o'clock. A very simple ceremony. We are not religious of course but we want a bond, and this is what is available now. The state refuses to allow us to marry. Can homosexuals marry in Ireland?'

'No,' said Nuala. ' Well, I don't think so.'

For Christ's sake? Ireland? Can gays marry in Ireland?

'You don't think so?' Elsa asked in her deep serious voice.

'I've never heard of…'

Erik turned from the sink. 'In Ireland,' he said in a blunt flat voice, 'homosexuality is against the law. So is heterosexuality, as far as I know.'

Elsa and Kirsten laughed heartily at his brilliantly original witticism, while Nuala wondered what the joke was, from their point of view. But of course she joined in the laughter. Just to be one of the crowd, just for politeness sake.

'Did you know this was all going on?'

Nuala and Erik were lying on her bed. The room was very warm and the light that fell across Erik's face was pink and gentle. Oh how romantic it was! Nothing like pink lights for encouraging love! But the narrowness of the bed had a familiar feel to it, and, even though the mattress was firm, not a spongy sack of blighted potatoes, they both felt very much at home.

'No, of course not,' Erik expostulated. 'Do you think I'd have come if I had known? Or invited you?'

'Well, why not? It's interesting. I mean of course it's all awfully weird and everything but that's what...Or is it? Does this sort of thing happen all the time here?'

'You know us. Brave little Denmark. Most liberal nation in the world. Birthplace of porn, home of contraception and every kind of vice.'

'I meant, do other people's mothers sort of take lesbian lovers and marry them?'

'I presume they do. The first part, anyway. Though actually I'd never come across it myself. And this marriage stuff is new. God, I don't know what they have to go and get married for. It's enough having that fat cow living here, living off Mother, without her being legally tied to her as well.'

'She's not fat. And it won't be legal, I gather.'

'Just you wait. I know Denmark.'

'Well, I can understand the urge to have a definite bond, a sort of official recognition of the relationship.'

Nuala brightened, pondering this new dimension of the problem. This marriage could be turned to her advantage, perhaps! A definite bond: that was what she was after, too. It was a natural and universal urge, after all, not some aberrant obsession which she should try to combat. Maybe Erik would understand that now?

'I can't,' said Erik gloomily. 'Most Danes, ordinary heterosexual Danes, don't get married.'

Nuala's heart sank again.

'They've given up on it; they want open, free relationships. It beats me why two middle-aged old women have to go and get something that ordinary people can't be bothered with any more. They are crazy. I come home for Christmas and my mother is gone crazy!'

'She seems sane enough to me. I don't know what you're worried about. I mean, if it's your inheritance or something I don't think there's likely to be a problem. It's not as if they were going to have kids, is it? And Elsa strikes me as the sort of woman who's very capable of supporting herself.'

'It would not surprise me if they did have kids. Nothing would surprise me now. There isn't much we can do about it anyway, is there?'

Come on Erik ! Don't fuss about nothing. Your mother's marrying her lover, so what?

'How would you feel if it was your mother?'

Mollie. Plump, round-faced, corkscrew perm. Plonked in front of the telly.

'Well…'

The image was a bit much. Nuala started to giggle. Erik, tossing his head in despair, started to giggle. They were soon rolling on the floor, in kinks, absolute kinks, of hilarity.

The next day was Christmas Eve, the day on which Christmas is celebrated in Denmark. When Nuala came downstairs, Kirsten and

Elsa, who were rarely seen apart, were in the kitchen having breakfast. The table was laid with a red cloth embroidered in white thread with reindeer, elves and stars. Among the plaited reed baskets of bread and Danish pastries small 'snowball' lights stood. It was still not light, and the candles flamed, feather lights in the morning dimness.

'Happy Christmas, Nuala!' Kirsten jumped up and kissed her. 'Come and join us for a Christmas breakfast. Erik is so lazy, he will not get up until lunchtime. That is the Irish habit, perhaps?'

Kirsten, Nuala immediately noticed, was wearing exactly what she had been wearing yesterday: a red jumper and red checked pants. Well, the colours were Christmasy, perhaps. But not much else. Elsa, one gathered on very little acquaintance with her, was the sort of woman who did not really care at all about clothes and always wore the same thing—blue jeans and a navy jumper. Nuala, in deference to the day that was in it, had on her burgundy velvet jacket, and black knickerbocker pants tucked into long leather boots. Her blouse was snow-white, copiously frilled, and had a small black bow at the neck.

'Happy Christmas,' she said unhappily, wishing she had waited for Erik. But they had not slept together; after being with her the night before, Erik had left her bed and gone to his own room, mainly from habit but also because the bed was too narrow. His own, Nuala had noted when she looked into the adjoining bedroom, was a double. They would use that in future, she decided.

'So Nuala, you have had some shocks since you came here, have you not?'

Kirsten spoke, but Elsa smiled and nodded in her superior way, and Nuala got the impression that she was speaking for the pair of them.

'Oh no. Of course not. I'm not shocked at all.'

Nuala took a pastry and cut it up, trying desperately to think of something intelligent to say.

'It does not surprise you that I am having a live-in lover, a gay lover?'

'Well, no...I mean I hadn't known about it, but of course it's perfectly all right with me.'

'Why shouldn't it be? It's none of your business.'

'Well no, it isn't.'

'I would like Nuala to understand the situation,' Kirsten turned rather coldly to Elsa. 'It is important to me that she understands.'

'I do understand,' said Nuala. Where the hell was Erik? He always got up early enough in Dublin.

'It is always so much better to talk about things, Nuala. We Danes like to bring things out into the open. We like to discuss things. It is a great national vice, discussing every little detail until everyone is bored to tears. Yes. But this is important to me.'

If she says that again I'll scream.

'It's important to me. You are a good friend of my son, yes? It is important to me that my son understands what is going on around here, you know, and that he accepts it, you know. He does not, I know it. I sense that he is uneasy at the moment. You know what I mean? I am right, eh?'

'Well…'

'Have some coffee, Nuala, and I will tell you everything.

Kirsten poured the coffee.

'Do try this cheese. It is low-fat; you do not have to worry about your figure.'

The knickerbockers make my bottom look enormous, I knew it.

'You take me, a woman aged forty-five, divorced for ten years. I am sick to the teeth of men. They are such cads, you know, the interesting ones. Or else they are boring or alcoholic or impotent or something is bound to be wrong. If I love them they leave me and if I do not love me they pursue me every minute of the day. I have had many relationships and I am sick of them, to the teeth. Every relationship with a man I have since I was sixteen has ended in war. It is war, what they say in the proverbs you know. A battlefield. So I am a pacifist, I am tired of going to the war, I will not go again, never again. So then I am alone. I am a doctor, I work hard in this big and, as you see, beautiful house. My child goes away to Ireland and never writes to me, hardly ever comes home on holidays. He is a man too, is he not? What should I expect? Then I join the women's group, the co-counselling, because I am sick of my therapist, I am sick of life. Right. I need help. And I get help. For the first time in twenty years I get help. I get love. From a woman. I do not have to fight about it. It is easy love. Is that wrong?'

'No...'

Put like that.

'Is it wrong that I should live with this woman who is my friend? Is it wrong that I should want to have an official ceremony, celebrating our love?'

'No, no.'

'You are a good girl, Nuala. But I know you have doubts. Listen, are you happy with Erik?'

'Well, yes, of course. I am...you know...yes, I am."

I love him. I love him. I love him so fucking much. Why can't I say it out loud? Why do I have to be ashamed of that?

'You are lying. Nobody will ever be happy with Erik. He is like his father. He and his father are the same person. They look the same, they talk the same, they dress the same. They are the same. They are afraid of women. I do not know why. Do you belong to a women's group, Nuala?'

'No.'
As a matter of fact I've never heard of a women's group.
'Join one.'
'I'm not sure if there are any at home.'
'There are women in Ireland too, I suppose?'
'Yes.'
'Do they all look like you?'
'What?'
The last questions had been Elsa's, not Kirsten's.
'Really Elsa! She is teasing you, Nuala. Do not mind Elsa. Her jokes, you know…'
She and Elsa were laughing.
'Dress like you, I mean, and have that hairstyle?'
'Most of them do, yes, mostly.' Nuala felt irritated now. Why should she have to look like them, that awful plain-Dane look? What was so wonderful about jeans and bobs.
'They will change,' said Elsa, 'when they get some sense.'

Nuala's immediate reaction to this conversation was to feel resentful and angry. Kirsten had gone too far, cross-examining her in that way, about such a subject. And on Christmas morning too! There was such a thing as a sense of timing. And what did it matter, what she thought about Kirsten and Elsa. If they wanted to behave like perfect fools they could jolly well put up with the consequences. (When Nuala got angry she reverted to schoolgirl slang, which she had learned from stories for girls when she was a child.) It was too much to expect everyone, even perfect strangers, to condone their carrying-on. Kirsten had been fishing for approval, it was as simple as that. All that stuff about being open and having a heart-to-heart discussion was rot, rotten rot. Rotten rotten rot.

Nuala was back in her room. She sat on the bed and scowled at the hessian floor. Should she get Erik? No, he would probably be as cranky as a barrel of rats at this hour. She got up and pulled back the curtains. The sun had risen now, and she was surprised to see that the garden and street outside were covered in a thick layer of snow. It sat like cotton wadding on the branches of the bare elms, and almost covered the red tiles of the houses.

She had never seen so much snow before.

She would have to get out in it.

Forget about Erik. Forget about Kirsten and Elsa. Forget everything except this white thing. This unexpected amazing wonderful perfect thing, this new lovely thing. The hush and the smooth of it, the cold and the glow of it.

What else matters right now?

On with the fake fur and Cossack hat, on with the red kid gloves, down the stairs and out the door and out into it.

Erik got up, finally, and Christmas Eve passed easily and enjoyably. There were guests for lunch, so Elsa and Kirsten were busy cooking all morning, while Nuala and Erik lolled in front of the aromatic log fire and listened to music or played the piano. Erik was rather good at it, and tried to teach Nuala, who was tone deaf, to play *Nu er det Jul igen*, a Danish Christmas carol. It took her over an hour to learn the simple tune, and in the end she played it in a plodding, incompetent manner. But with a great sense of achievement.

Lunch was traditional, and very good: roast pork, carmelised potatoes, red cabbage. It was all accompanied by large quantities of wine or beer, and every two minutes or so someone proposed a toast and everyone had to drink snaps—a horrible drink which burned Nuala's throat. The guests, two couples (heterosexual) and the hostesses became merrier and merrier as the meal progressed and more and more glasses of snaps were disposed of. Toasts were drunk, to Nuala, to Erik, to Nuala and Erik, to the guests and, of course, to Elsa and Kirsten and their happy future.

Erik played *Que sera sera* and sang to his own accompaniment.

'You are much better than Doris Day, Erik!' said Elsa, patting him—or was it thumping him—on the back. 'And I get the message, I hope.'

He looked at her sourly and continued to thump the piano.

'Erik has difficulty in coming to terms with my liaison with Kirsten,' Elsa turned and anounced haughtily to the assembled company. 'I know he will deny it but it is true.'

Erik continued to play, although his face darkened perceptibly. Kirsten looked warningly at Elsa and the guests, who had been chatting to Nuala, fell suddenly silent and started critically at the speaker. Their faces, which had been animated and charming a second before, now reminded Nuala of classical statues, or of models in glossy advertisements: they stared coldly and superciliously past Elsa, their eyes trained on some distant, inhuman horizon. Stones, they were, or Medusas, hoping to freeze Elsa into silence.

She was probably very hot-blooded, like a lot of people with an exaggerated sense of their own importance.

'Why should we pretend with one another? Kirsten and I are in love; we are going to get married. But Erik disapproves, and you disapprove. I can sense it in the air. Disapprobation is thick in the atmosphere. It is drowning the candles and the paper hearts; even the red cabbage and the roast pork are swimming in it. It is choking me. Why are we all so dishonest?'

Nobody spoke; nobody even shifted in their chair. It was so embarrassing.

'We are supposed to be a liberal, tolerant society here. But I don't think we are, I don't think its true. And I don't like that. I don't like hypocrisy. You are all whited sepulchres.'

Suddenly it dawned on them all at once: Elsa was drunk. The knowledge defrosted everyone. Kirsten came over and put her arm around Elsa, patting her on the shoulder and saying, 'Sit down, my dear. Sit in this chair here.' The guests giggled a little shyly, shrugged their shoulders and went back to their conversation for a few minutes before saying they had to go. Erik and Nuala went to the kitchen to do the washing-up, embarrassed on account of the guests but vaguely pleased that Elsa, Big Miss Know-It-All, had made a bit of an eejit of herself.

CHAPTER NINE

The wedding was a pleasant and uneventful affair. There were very few guests, but those present looked exactly like guests at any nuptial celebration: men dressed in dark suits, women in pastel coats and dresses. Since Elsa wore a tuxedo and Kirsten an off-white dress and a large orange hat, it was easy to forget the exceptional character of the event. Moreover, the ceremony was mercifully brief.

The reception, held at a restaurant in Helsingor, looking out over the frozen sea, was more like a pleasant family dinner party than a wedding. Amid the pink carnations and Christmas decorations, suspension of disbelief was no problem, as far as Nuala and most of those present were concerned. For Erik, it was a different and more difficult story. But he did not bother Nuala with details of his trauma. People's traumas are not all that interesting to third parties, once they have been described once or twice.

Nuala's week flew by: Erik treated her in gentlemanly fashion even after his mother and Elsa had left them alone in the Charlottenlund house to go on their honeymoon to Thailand. She had anticipated that his attitude would undergo a transformation as soon as they departed, but no. Although he was perhaps less clinging, less dependent on her than he had been initially, he played the part of host with some spirit. To her surprise—because in Ireland he had been rather lazy—he took it upon himself to show all the most significant sights in Copenhagen and the surrounding district. She went to Tivoli, to the Little Mermaid, to Helsingor, properly, to look at the castle, to all the best Copenhagen churches, to the Thorvaldsen museum and the Royal Library and the Museum of Modern Art at Louisiana. They took the train to Roskilde to look at the cathedral where the kings and queens of Denmark lie buried, and to the Viking ships that are restored in a glass showcase overlooking the sea there. They even went to Malmö, in Sweden, on a day trip. In the evenings there were shows at the ballet and the opera, and dinners in elegant half-empty restaurants. What there was not were many friends. Did Erik have any? She did not enquire. She was just as pleased to be alone with him anyway, having a good time. Alone, that is, in public places. He kept her so busy that there was hardly a single moment when they were not out somewhere. By the time they returned home at night, they were totally exhausted: the romantic interludes of Nuala's first days in Copenhagen were not repeated. And she did not really miss them. Erik was doing his job much too well for that.

At the end of the week, sated with views and museums and new experiences, she flew back to Dublin as she had flown out. Alone.

Alone. What Nuala did not like to be.

The flight was not bad. Flying was still a novelty for her; she still liked funny little meals packed in plastic trays and enjoyed browsing through the brochure, wondering if she should buy a silk scarf with a design of horses on it for thirty pounds, or imitation gold earclips. The many pages advertising various kinds of perfume she passed over quickly. They were outrageously expensive, and since she had never even smelt any of these fashionable perfumes in her life she could not imagine why anyone would buy them. Her eyes lingered momentarily on the picture of Chanel Number 5. Was that the perfume Marilyn Monroe mentioned in some line or other? 'I'll wear nothing except Chanel Number 5!' She wouldn't have minded trying that; the association with Marilyn Monroe appealed to her, as well as the association with Chanel. Nuala loved anything that suggested Paris or chic.

Distracted by such musings, she managed to forget that she was sad to leave Erik and for some reason uneasy about him, even though they had been getting on so well. Separation. She distrusted it. So far Erik had always come back to her after holidays. But she still knew they were danger spots. If someone was feeling dubious about their partner, all their doubts would have time to fester and come to a head during a spell apart. She had often noticed it; in college the great breaking-up time had been after the summer holidays.

Nuala always hated coming home to Dublin. Abroad was so much nicer. She hated it now, thudding sickeningly against the rainwashed runway, running from one expanse of murky sky to another.

How bleak is my city.

The way in from the airport. What a welcome to our green and pleasant land. Ballymun. Whitehall. Drumcondra. Dorset Street, Gardiner Street, the back of Summerhill. Slums and factories and the north side. The best bit is Griffith Avenue and even that bears a strong resemblance to a graveyard. It's a wonder they didn't put the airport in the middle of Glasnevin cemetery.

I want to die. I want to die when I see all this, when I see Mollie and Dessie and the orange and lime-green and brown nylon carpet in the hall. Lurid isn't the word. And those brass ducks flying up the walls. And the blare of the telly and the coldness of my room.

Why is Ireland such a poor shabby place?

How can Erik take me seriously, a person who lives in a dump like this? A Turk in Copenhagen would deride it. The difference, the difference ! Ah, woe is me.

'Did you have a great time?'

Give them the whiskey and run. I can't talk to them, my tongue is tied, I hate it all too much. I've got to get out of this dive, I've got to. I'm sorry folks but I'm disowning yez all now after me week abroad! Yes I'm disowning you my family and my country, my native land. I don't want it. I want frozen sea and snow in my garden and pickled herrings on my plate, yes, I want all that and a hot hot house and Habitat furniture and I want luxury and well-being and a rich social welfare state.

Erik means all that to me. He's not just a fellow; he's a continent. I've got to have him, I've got to have a European. I've got to have a Dane who's my passport to all that. Who needs a mother and father, if they've got Denmark?

She cried that night, Nuala did, in her cold empty room (Mary wasn't there of course. Out screwing John Smyth as usual). Sobs, big gusty ones, into her flat feather pillow, the white pillowcase so ancient that it was nearly transparent, the stripes of the pillow showed right through it, little soft feathers creeping through thin bits and getting into her nose as she sobbed her heart out. Not for Erik. For Denmark, or what might have been. For Nuala, the Nuala there would have been if she'd been born in Charlottenlund and not Rathmines. If she'd been born in Foxrock and not Exeter Place. Oh, woe, woe.

Think of the black babies.

Think of the black hole of Calcutta.

Think of Pol Pot.

The thoughts that cheer. Ah yes but. Think of Erik, on his tod in the drawing room over there, the curtains drawn against the snowy garden. The stereo crooning out his favourite old classicals. A great man for the Mozart, Erik, morning, noon and night the sweet notes filled the air of that house. The carnations wilting a little now on the rosewood table. The rugs slightly crumpled on the nut-shiny floor.

Outside there the stars. The frozen sea. The children skating on the frozen ponds. The mums and dads skiing on the flat plains to the north of the city. So, that sort of cross-country skiing is hard work. It's fun too. It's more fun than cross-country walking in the bleeding rain. It's dry, it's white, it's glittering, it's festive. It's life.

Work came into its own that week, the week before Erik came back. The office, normally such a pain in the neck, such a huge non-event, became more than bearable. Sean and Tommy with their stupid goings on seemed not idiots but friends, warm humane companionable creatures, practical men who just wanted to have a bit of a lark, to make all their fellow humans face life with a smile.

They had decorated the office for Christmas. Long red paper chains were draped over the filing cabinets, trailing down and across the floor.

'Modern art!' said Tommy gleefully. 'We don't need any of that conventional old stuff in here; we want to be more abstract and expressive.'

He put sprigs of holly behind everyone's ears. He tied a tinsel rope across the doorway, so that people coming in or out had to jump over it or crawl underneath.

Bloody slapstick, childish, stupid, silly, Nuala had thought, before she went to Denmark. Now it seemed gay...no no try another word...cheery, positive, light-hearted, benign. When people tripped over the tinsel, she laughed louder than anyone.

One morning, she came in ten minutes late and disgruntled. When you were late, someone put a red 'x' beside your name in the attendance book. If you got seven 'x's, you received a letter, warning you about them. If you got fourteen 'x's, you lost your increment for that year. You also endangered your chances of promotion: one colleague of Nuala's had lost all his increments for ten years and several opportunities for promotion on account of the number of 'x's after his name, referred to, in tones of mock-despair, as 'Billy's lates'. Even though he was one of the most talented civil

servants in the department, it made no
difference; promotion depended almost entirely
on being in time in the morning, as far as she
could gather. Even though she did not intend to
stay in the job Nuala hated getting 'x's. She felt
the same about them as she did about getting
slaps in school. The slaps didn't hurt much in
themselves but they were unbearably
humiliating. A sign that, when it came to the
crunch, you were without any power.

Tommy met her as she climbed angrily over
the tinsel.

'Guess what?' he asked in his quick excited
voice. 'Sean's engaged. I'm going to tell Mr
Byrne.'

And he was off, like a messenger from the
gods, to spread the news.

Sean was standing by his desk, his duffle-
coat still on, grinning in a proud, shy manner.

'Congratulations, Sean!' Nuala said. 'I hope
you'll be very happy.'

'Thanks,' he replied, and did not expand. He
was still smiling. His face looked like a very
small boy's, round and red, when he smiled.

'It's great news,' Nuala gushed on, because
the silence was heavy, somehow, and Tommy
was not there to lighten it with his pranks. 'I'm
really glad to hear it. When did you decide?'

'Over the Christmas,' he said. 'Over the
turkey and ham and the plum pud, you know,
when most people decide. We've been going
together for a year now, you know, and I'm

nearly twenty-two. It's getting to that time of life…no point in waiting till I'm an old man, is there?'

'Oh no, no,' agreed Nuala. No no. I'm twenty-two too, I'm twenty-two too, and I'm waiting, I'm waiting to be an old woman, aren't I? 'You're doing the right thing. It's wonderful, it's just wonderful.'

It's a miracle, that's what it is. Young Man Volunteers to Marry Young Woman. Three-inch headlines. Hear Ye, Hear Ye, Young Men of Ireland and Denmark. It is OK to get married. It is normal. Sean is doing it of his own free will, and him not twenty-three. Christ is risen. The Blessed Virgin is dancing the dance of the seven veils in the garden of Gethsemane.

'I really think its good news. Say so to Jenny.'

Jenny was his fiancée.

Tommy was overjoyed too. He was a married man himself. In the evenings, when the others went for a jar, he drove home to Shankill, to his wife and two kids. Even on special occasions, Christmas or birthdays or engagements or resignations, he did not come to the pub, but hastened to the bosom of his family in their semi-d. Welcome to the club, Sean, it's a laugh all the way after this. Mortgage. ESB bill. New winter coats for the kiddies. Piano lessons. Orthodontic treatment. Braces, violins, bottles, bottled gas, rolling down the lanes of your future.

'When's the big day?'

'March,' said Sean flatly. 'The day after Patrick's Day'

'Super! We're all invited, I suppose.'

'That's up to Jenny. Her da's footing the bill.'

They all sat down then. His voice seemed tired and sick of it all. They sat down at their tinsel-draped desks, opened their files and fiddled with them. And another day passed.

After work, a visit to O'Dwyer's to celebrate the engagement was more or less obligatory. Nuala went, and drank several jars and it was almost midnight when she reached home. Dessie and Mollie were asleep: they went to bed before twelve as a rule, since Dessie had to get up at seven for his job. He always started work at eight o clock.

In the sitting room, huddled over the fire, she found Mary, whom she had not encountered since before her trip to Denmark. She poked at the embers to encourage them to glow but the fire was almost out, and it was obvious that Mary, too, had come in quite recently.

'Hello, stranger.' Nuala used an idiomatic expression she would have shunned had she not drunk five glasses of Harp. But the expression was apt; Mary had all but officially moved away from home now. Some of her clothes hung in the wardrobe but they were being removed, piece by piece. Most of her books were still stacked on the rickety shelves she'd made herself the year she did the Leaving. A few personal effects—a half-empty bottle of cologne, a powder puff, a needle stuck into a spool of yellow thread—lingered on the dressing table, mementoes of a former worshipper at its foxy mirror. Mollie had at last stopped keeping dinners hot for her, a practice she had been loath to give up, but, after months of throwing away dried-up peas and leathery slices of bacon, she had been forced to face reality.

'Hello.' Mary smiled winsomely, as was her way. 'How was Denmark?'

'Wonderful, absolutely wonderful!' Nuala said enthusiastically. 'You must go there, sometime. You'd just adore it!'

'I must do that,' she said distantly. For a few minutes she stared into the fire. Then all of a sudden she burst into tears. Oh Christ, thought Nuala, I'm off. It was not that Mary never cried. Like many highly-strung, ruthless women, she did so quite frequently: it was as if all her tenseness, beauty like a tautened bow etc etc, suddenly slackened terribly for one reason or another and she broke down, just to give herself a break, a bit of relief. Then she would tighten herself right back up again and go back to being taut and ruthless all over again.

'Oh goodness, what's wrong?' Nuala did not know how to cope. She was tired and drunk. She had just come home from Denmark, a lesbian wedding and a diffident lover, to rain in

Rathmines and engagements in the office. And now this.

Mary sobbed. Big gusty babyish sobs.

'Can I get you something? A cup of tea?'

Shake of the head.

'Brandy?'

Nod of the head. Oh, of course. Over Nuala tottered to the cocktail cabinet, a ghastly teak cabinet Mollie had bought before Christmas. It was like a closed-up, stripy bureau, but when you let down the lid you found a formica and mirror-lined compartment, filled with bottles and glasses. With difficulty Nuala located the brandy she had purchased at Kastrup, and poured two generous glasses. She couldn't find brandy glasses so she used tumblers instead, fat short ones decorated with little green shamrocks.

She managed to carry them across the room without any disasters, and as soon as she was comfortably seated she began to pry.

'So what's the matter? Is it John?'

'Yes, yes. Of course it is.'

'You've broken up?'

'Oh no. No. Nothing as stupid as that, no.'

That's the kind of stupid thing that can only happen to twits like me.

'Well, what then?'

'It's all so complicated. You have no idea.'

'No,' said Nuala, getting up from the mat and sitting in her mother's fireside chair, which was soft and comfortable. Mary blew her nose.

This seemed a favourable sign.

'What's so complicated about it?' Nuala ventured.

'Well, you see, we want to get married.'

'I see,' said Nuala, taking a deep draught. Was that complicated?

'The problem being, he's married already.'

'Mm.' Sure, every Tom, Dick and Harry knows that.

'Nobody realises it, you see. He's been separated for years and years; he was only married for a short time anyway. But you can see that it's going to be tricky for us. With no divorce legislation or anything.'

'You can get one abroad, can't you? I'm always hearing about foreign divorces.' Nuala spoke cheerily, trying to be uplifting.

'Well, maybe…I don't know how to go about it. It's all so complicated.'

To Nuala's horror, she started to weep again.

'The real problem is not so much that.'

Sob sob. Oh mother of God. Don't tell me she's pregnant.

'It's my thesis.'

'Your thesis?'

'Yes.'

Sob sob sob sob.

'You're not working on it, is that it?'

'No, not really. I mean, I do do it. I do get time and I work at it quite a lot. Actually, its finished. I've finished the first draft now.'

'Well, isn't that good?'

'He doesn't like it.'

'Mm.' Was this such a disaster? Apparently so.

'You see, he used to think it was good but now he doesn't. He thinks it's awful. He thinks he made a mistake about me, thought I was better than I really am.'

'But that's silly, Mary. Everyone knows you're good. You've always been clever and so on.'

'I used to be. But now I'm not. I've lost my touch or something. He wants me to give it up.'

'The creep!'

Nuala hadn't, of course, read the thesis, and had no intention of doing so. God, it would be worse than reading people's poetry, and being asked what did you think! But Mary had been working at this thing for three years. It couldn't be all that awful.

'He says it's hopeless. A complete waste of time. He says if I submit it it's bound to fail, and he can't help me because of our emotional involvement. It's all going to cause all sorts of terrible problems.'

'Well, didn't you think of that at first?'

'Well, yes. We sort of thought it might work out. But now I've got to make my choice. Him or the thesis. Oh it's so awful, it's just awful!'

'It is, all right.' Nuala's head was spinning, and she felt the beginning of a ghastly headache. The beer, the brandy, now this. Why hadn't Mary stayed away from this person who was old enough to be her father? Why did she have to make such a mess of a perfectly good life, the enviable life she'd had?

'Well, seeing as he can't marry you...' she said, in tones which were becoming slurred.

'He wants to marry me. He thinks it will all work out.'

'For him,' said Nuala, bitterly. 'Look, why don't you just give him up? It's the obvious thing to do.'

She started crying again.

'I can't give him up. I love him. I can't give him up now.'

I know the feeling.

'Goodnight. I've got to get some sleep.'

'Goodnight.'

The next day was dreadful. Erik's plane was due in at nine o'clock in the morning, and every time Nuala's phone rang, she was sure it was going to be him. But it never was. She decided that she would definitely not phone him first. She wanted to prove that she had some pride left. Besides, things had gone so well in Copenhagen: Erik had seemed to need her, almost to love her, during that unusual week. At least at the beginning...Although when she thought of it he hadn't been especially affectionate over the last four or five days. Still, he had been most attentive to her needs, making every effort to see that she had a holiday full of fun and variety, as travel brochures put it. If there was any logic in sexual relationships, or in Erik, he would be at least as anxious to get in touch with her as she with him. He would certainly phone as soon as he landed or at least as soon as he arrived at the flat.

She hung on till eleven. Well, it takes about two hours to get from the airport to Rathmines, if you use buses. Any time now. She waited till twelve. It's winter. Time of fog, frost, snow. Delays of all kinds. Looking at the clear blue sky, feeling the noonday sun warming her cheeks, she waited till one. Then she phoned.

He didn't have a phone of his own in the flat, but shared a communal coinbox with all the residents of the house. So you always had to wait for a long time before anyone answered it. It rang and it rang. She could hear its high rings resonating through the big, and, it seemed, empty house. After about five minutes of this, someone lifted the receiver.

'Hello!' said a deep foreign accent. Foreign, but not Danish.

'I'd like to speak to Erik Andersen please. He's in the top front room.'

'What name you say?'

'Erik Andersen.'

'Repeat for me, please.'

Nuala repeated.

'Spell please.'

Nuala spelt.

'One moment. I try bell.'

She heard bells ringing faintly. Buzz. Buzz. She held her breath and her heart. Everything inside her tightened and her mind was blank.

'Hello!'

'Hello.'

The elastic snaps.

'Sorry, no answer.'

'Thank you very much. Goodbye.'

Voice tiny, dry with disappointment.

'You try again later.'

There was sympathy in the deep rich voice. As if it wasn't bad enough...

'Goodbye.'

She slammed down the receiver.

Don't cry.

She sat at her desk right through lunch-hour, unable to muster up the energy to go out and eat, to go for a walk. At two o'clock, she asked Tommy if she could go home. She pleaded illness. He was very concerned.

'Go home now, and get a hot water bottle and a glass of honey and lemon, and spend the rest of the day in bed. Honey and lemon's the best thing for that old flu, isn't it, Sean?'

'Honey and lemon's the man,' Sean said, smiling sympathetically at Nuala.

She felt momentarily comforted, as if they had poured honey and lemon over her frantic heart and soothed it for a moment or two. In an unusually frank outburst, she grasped Tommy's hand and said, 'Thanks a lot. I'll probably be OK tomorrow.'

For a split second, the thought of home and honey and lemon and a nice rest in bed, seemed more attractive than the possibly bleak alternative. A little bout of flu, even a little stay in hospital, would have its appeal. Even a little break in a comfortable prison might be preferable to having to face the difficult reality of life with Erik. It was a hard station, as her father, or brother, would have put it. Only the prospect of life without Erik seemed worse.

Putting these distracting thoughts from her mind, she galloped off at full speed to Frankfurt Avenue. She rang the bell with a sense of foreboding. In less than a minute, the door was opened and Erik stood on the threshold.

'Hey there.' He smiled in a sweet and polite and civilised fashion.

'Hi!' said Nuala, cheerily. No one could have guessed from her tone and her demeanour that five minutes before she had been on the verge of a nervous breakdown. As soon as she saw his friendly expression, she swiftly brushed her own apprehensions under the carpet and pretended to be in the best of good humour. She was—sometimes, for as long as she could stand it—no more than a mirror reflecting Erik's mood. 'How are you?' she said, kissing him companionably on the cheek. 'I took the afternoon off, to see you!'

'That is great,' Erik said. But not enthusiastically enough for Nuala. She felt her anxiety return, an icy tooth chewing at the bottom of her stomach. 'Come in.'

The flat was warm, for once: after Denmark, Erik was being generous with the electricity. And there were some other mementoes of the holiday, some additional comforts: a new rug on the floor, fluffy towels hanging on the back of a chair and a wonderful new duvet on the bed. The flat looked cosier and prettier than it ever had done. And what was that on the bedside table? A little white box with black-and-gold borders. Chanel No 5! Nuala's heart opened and she smiled warmly at Erik. How stupid she had been to doubt him! Stupid and, what was worse, disloyal.

There was a bottle of *snaps* lying on the bed, in its bag. He hadn't really finished unpacking. Obviously he had just arrived.

'Like a drink?' he offered in a kind but brittle voice.

'Yes please.' Nuala smiled again and stretched in the one big armchair. It was not often that Erik had drink on offer in the bedsit. She couldn't remember when they had ever drunk anything that she hadn't brought there herself. Erik was a bit puritanical and a bit unromantic and maybe just a little bit mean, too, when it came to things like offering people drinks.

'Here, look at this,' he said, to her surprise, handing her a chapter of his thesis. 'Could you read it and tell me what you think?'

'Of course, I'd be glad to,' said Nuala,

puzzled now. This was truly an *embarras de richesses*. Perfume, alcohol and a request for advice all in one go. Where was it all going to end?

She began to skim through the first page:

'Any study of Chaucer's style can be approached from a number of angles. For example, the text may be examined in isolation, according to the practices of the now rather obsolete school of new criticism. Or it can be surveyed from an historical point of view. This approach is becoming popular among modern Chaucerian scholars and is...'

'So, what do you think?'

Erik handed her a tumbler holding a thimbleful of *snaps*.

'Thank you,' said Nuala. 'I've just read the first paragraph, really. It seems super, though. I'd really like to read it all.'

So where is the perfume?

'Thanks,' said Erik. 'Cheers!' He raised his glass.

'Cheers,' said Nuala. She glanced over at the bedside table. The white-black-and-gold box had disappeared.

She knocked back the whole tumbler of the revolting liquor and let it burn her throat.

Maybe he had it in his pocket. Maybe he was going to give it to her later, a big surprise to gladden her heart later on today, or later on tomorrow, or some other day.

Maybe he was.

CHAPTER TEN

And maybe he wasn't.

He said nothing and for a while Nuala held back the tide of her suspicions and jealousy. But eventually she lost the battle. Erik's behaviour spoke louder than words and kept her swinging from nervous hope to turbulent anguish: he was late for every appointment or else he just didn't turn up at all. When they were together he was inattentive or critical. His eyes always seemed to be elsewhere than on her—often they were on whatever clock happened to be closest, or he sneaked glances at his watch every two minutes. In her rational moments, which were not very numerous, she wondered why he did not just tell her. But he didn't. And in one of *her* rational moments, after a particularly bad night of stomach churning and heart battering, she told him.

'You're so possessive, Nuala. I do not understand it,' said Erik. He was standing in the hall of the house at Exeter Place, the very spot where it had all begun.

'I am possessive; I know that,' she said. 'That's the way I am.'

Your mother is married to her girlfriend.

149

Your father ran off to marry a colleague. You should know something about the nature of possessiveness. I'm possessive because I'm in love with you. That's the way people are; it's not just me. She thought but did not express. She did not feel like expressing anything, this cold moment in the hall. The moment she had been dreading and trying to prevent ever since she'd met Erik. And it was as boring as it was painful. The only thing she wanted was that it should be over. There was no point in holding on to Erik now, holding on to the Erik who did not love her but loved someone else. The only thing to do now was let him go and open the next page.

'Yes…You know, I think we should have a greater variety of friends. We are young. We should be having a good time and a lot of experiences. That is what I feel but I have never been able to convince you of it.'

'No.'

Most unsatisfactory, she knew, her response. Erik wanted an argument. He wanted to stay on the doorstep, fighting with her in to the night. He wasn't going to love her, he wasn't going to give up Vogue, he wasn't ready for any sort of commitment. But he didn't want to lose her either, right now. She saw this. Her love for him had been assaulted so strongly, though, that she was bitter and pessimistic. Tomorrow he would be as bad as ever if she gave him another chance.

'Well, yes.' He frowned, and pulled at the
zip of his parka. 'Well, of course I do not want a
complete break...I want us to be friends, you
know. To meet from time to time.'

Funny how words like 'friend' and 'meet
from time to time' make you feel physically
wounded. He was walloping her with them.
Take that! 'Friendship'. Slam bash! 'Keep in
touch!'

'Yes, that's all right.'

'Well...goodbye.'

'Goodbye.'

It was still difficult to get him out of the
door, to get rid of him entirely. But eventually
he left, so obviously distraught by guilt that
Nuala felt sorry for him. She did not watch him
walk to the gate but shut the door as soon as he
stepped over the threshold and ran upstairs to
bed.

She felt more tired than she had ever felt in
her life before.

That was the easy part.

During the two or three days that followed,
the torturer worked on her. She felt herself
successively flayed and disembowelled, racked
and pressed. She'd gone through this physical
stuff before, quite often, during the past while.
She'd almost learned to detach her mind from
the upheaval that heartbreak was able to cause
in her body. But she'd never had to put up with
this for such long stretches of time. In the past,
a few hours or even a day of fretting—isn't that

what any sensible person, the sort of practical person who tells silly girls like Nuala to pull themselves together, would call this?—would always be cured by the eventual encounter with Erik. In his arms, or even talking to him for five minutes on the phone, the anxiety would disappear, and afterwards Nuala would forget all about it, as they say women forget the pains of labour as soon as the child is born.

This was a long labour. The child would not be born.

The first stage finished after three days, and a new phase commenced. The unbearable lightness of being phase. Her own arms and hands and legs seemed new, like fragile and vulnerable extensions, pins affixed to her body, false, strange. Her insides felt hollow. She was a shell, paper-thin, featherlight. Her head was dizzy.

The hardest part was when all the physical activity was over. That in its own unpleasant way had been preoccupying. Suffering is demanding. You know it is an enemy and you are kept busy, battling with it. You are heartened occasionally by small triumphs. The hardest bit was when she was no longer fighting the turmoil and tears that her body produced just as it occasionally produced headaches or stomach cramps. The hardest bit came after all that, during the convalescence stage, when her body was calm and the action moved into her mind.

Today there will be no Erik.

Today stretches ahead, empty and without any meaning.

I have work I am not interested in. I have no lover. I am nothing.

Alas and alack.

She tripped lightly to work, like a fairy, like a ghost.

She carried out her tasks at the office in a new, careful manner, as if she were treading on eggshells all the time. And everything she touched seemed to have acquired a new quality, a new personality. Like her, the pens and the files and the brochures seemed to be fresh and delicate, baby-soft baby-light objects, which had to be handled with skill and caution, in case they would break. And she was conscious herself of being breakable, too. As long as she continued carefully, avoiding the cracked place, she would be all right. Eyes averted, stare straight ahead. If she lost her footing, took a false step, she would be lost, carried away screaming in a strait-jacket.

Oddly, it seemed to her that Tommy and Sean and everyone at the office knew exactly what had happened. As if they had been hiding in the garden hedge, witnessing the leave-taking. Or had Erik, who hardly knew them, telephoned the exciting news to them early in the morning, before Nuala had come in? Surely, surely, they were nothing as interesting and exotic as telepathic? Yet this seemed to be the only explanation for their kind, considerate treatment of her. There was no teasing or ragging this morning. Tommy had told her in warm and genuine-sounding tones that her blouse was lovely and Sean had sat beside her at tea break and chatted, instead of rushing off to play Twenty-five with some other fellows, as he usually did. Even Pauline, the engaged, the aloof and, Nuala had discovered, the stingy, had demonstrated extraordinary concern by offering her a chocolate éclair (the sweet, not the cake, kind). Nuala accepted it, although the last thing she wanted was sweets. But she was afraid to reject such an exceptional gesture. It might have been unlucky.

She had arranged to meet Jean for lunch about a week after the split. It would have been pleasant to avoid meeting anyone, to avoid lunch altogether. In her condition, eating seemed gross and inappropriate. But she never broke lunch appointments, unless there was a very good reason (such as being called upon by Erik at the last minute). So at one o'clock she trotted along—glided along—to Jonathan's, their habitual lunching place.

She did not tell Jean about the change in her situation. Indeed, she realised as she sat encased in her lime-green chair, eating moussaka at a white plastic table, she did not want to tell anyone about it. She did not want to talk about Erik at all. When Jean asked her how he was, she said fine, which was no doubt true.

Jean gave a fairly detailed account of the wedding.

'She was quite noticeable,' she said, picking at her Russian salad. 'But nice, in a báinín dress and jacket, with a purple hat. It sounds funny, but it suited her somehow.'

'And did you enjoy the whole thing? Was it fun?'

'Oh yes, it was very nice in a way. Nice food and things you know, it being in her own house. Her mother did it all. God, all the work, I don't know how she did it single-handed. I wouldn't like to do it myself, I really wouldn't. I'd get in caterers. It's dear, I know, but let's face it, it's only once in a lifetime, isn't it? She was great, her mother. She didn't seem put out, or anything; she was really great. I don't know how my mother would feel in that situation, I really don't. I mean, my mother is the most broadminded person you could meet, she really is. But I don't know how she'd feel if I suddenly announced I was pregnant and going to get married. I wouldn't like to have to do it.'

'No.'

Jean was looking perkier than usual. Her curls had been newly washed, or done at the hairdressers, or something, and her eyes sparkled. Something was up.

'Anything new with you?'

'Well…I've been to Denmark, did I tell you

about that?'

'No. How was it?'

'Oh, wonderful. Very nice and beautiful and luxurious and so on, you know. I'd a great time.'

She did not feel like describing the holiday in greater detail, although it would have been interesting to see Jean's reactions to the story of Erik's mother.

'That's good.' Jean didn't care about Denmark, Nuala could see that. She was bursting with her own good fortune, whatever it was. But then, she always seemed to be bursting with good fortune: she was a very positive person, Jean.

'I've got a bit of news,' Jean said with a grin.

'Oh?'

Not her. She couldn't be. Of all people.

'I'm getting married in June.'

Oh that. The only other bit of news there is, nowadays, it seems. Preggers or marriage, or both.

'Well that's absolutely marvellous,' cried Nuala. 'I hope you'll be very happy.'

'Thank you,' she grinned. 'We've had a stroke of luck, actually.'

'Oh?'

'We've put a deposit on a house. It's not quite ready yet but it will be by June.'

'Wonderful! Did someone leave you money or something?'

Jean's mouth pursed up and her face closed

like a clam. She did not like to divulge the nuts and bolts of her economy. That was her own business. Nuala had such bad judgement; anyone could see she was basically a guttersnipe.

A few seconds passed before her mouth opened again, and she was off.

'Something like that. The house is in Dundrum, in a place called Wedgwood. It's very nice, very nice indeed. It's a quiet little cul-de-sac, you know, not a boring cul-de-sac. I always think cul-de-sacs are boring, don't you, they're nice, and they're lovely and safe if you've got children, and they're quiet, but they can be just a little bit boring. At least that's what I think, I don't know what you think but that's what I think. But this cul-de-sac is different, it really is, it's an interesting cul-de-sac, it's got lots of big mature trees all along the path and the houses are spaced out nicely, it's really nice.'

'Dundrum is convenient.'

'Yes, it's a good location. Property values will increase there, so it's a sound investment. I don't think investment is the only thing you should be thinking of when you're buying a home; after all other factors may be more important, like whether you like the place or not. But we do like it, we really do, we really love it. And let's face it, it's the biggest investment we'll ever make, it's the biggest investment most people make in their lifetimes, so it is important to make sure it's a sound one. I know some people might think I'm being mercenary or something, but I'm not. I'm just facing facts, it's the biggest investment I'll ever make in my whole life, it really is, and I want it to be a sound one, I think that's sensible, not mercenary.'

Oh great. Investments. Money in bricks and mortar. The foundations of a life laid. The dynasty begins.

'Why don't we have a glass of wine, to celebrate?'

Nuala ordered two glasses of white wine, and even managed to clink them together joyfully, and make a sort of *ad hoc* toast to Jean and her house in Wedgwood and her future with her husband to be, Cyril whom Nuala hadn't seen for years, because Erik hadn't approved of him. Then they went window shopping and this time looked at material for wedding dresses: June planned to make her own, because that would be more satisfactory in the end, she thought. When miles of taffeta and lace and silk and satin, in all possible permutations of white, off-white, on-white, green-white, blue-white, soft white, true white, snow-white, ice-white, apple-white, orange-white had been examined, and Nuala was suffering from snow-blindness—on top of everything else—they parted. Just as she was going, Jean said, 'By the way, I'm going to a lecture in Fairfield next week, something you might be interested in. It's on alternative lifestyles. The Women's Group, you know. I go there occasionally.'

'Who's giving it?'

The Women's Group. Where have I heard that before? And since when did women who are just about to get married go to women's groups anyway?

'Somebody called Lane Brown,' she said. 'An American or a Canadian or something. A friend of mine is involved in the organisation of it. Catherine Hickey. Do you know her? No. She did Social Science. That's why I'm going.'

'I'll think about it. I'll give you a ring.'

That evening, at the dinner table, Nuala said to her mother, 'I'm going to get a flat.'

Mollie looked up from her plate, which had two red roses painted on the rim and one slice of cold roast beef, a mound of pale green chopped cabbage and a potato reclining in the middle.

'Oh? Is that so?'

'Yes,' said Nuala, in tones which were very shaky. She had decided to broach this subject while the iron was hot, in the hope that courage would not fail her as she knew it would do if she stopped to consider her plans. But now it was failing, very rapidly. There was so little of it, not nearly enough to last an entire meal with Mollie. Dessie was not present; he was working overtime.

'Yeah,' she continued. 'I've decided to try living alone for a while. I'm twenty-two already, after all.'

'Hmm'

'It's not that I don't like being here or anything,' she lied. 'It's more a matter of wanting to be independent. I think that's important, really. It's just—' she floundered on, getting deeper and deeper into a morass of apology, '—it's just a sort of experiment, you know. I mean I'll probably try it for a while, and then move back.'

Qui s'excuse, s'accuse. But she knew Mollie's attitude to children, which was basically that they were like government investment bonds. You bought them early in life and then waited patiently for the dividends. Children were a big investment, like the bonds that could only be bought if you had a thousand pounds minimum. But the interest was high. They would stay with you, live with you, buy you thirty-inch television sets and deep freezes for Christmas, look after you in your old age. Especially if they happened to be daughters. Mollie was adaptable. But it was hard to change overnight a way of thinking that had centuries of tradition behind it, just because your daughter happened to have gone to college and got fancy notions above her station. Yes, Mollie thought in terms of station. She'd been trying to get above her own all her life; she'd pushed Nuala and Mary and Christopher above theirs. But that didn't make it easier to accept the ideas that came with the station.

'I see,' said Mollie, pouting. Really Nuala was as odd as two boots since she started that old Civil Service job. She should never have taken it. With her qualifications! All that Erik fella's fault. Nuala had no sense of reality. Obsessed with boys she was, ever since she'd left school. What made them think that marriage was the be-all and end-all of existence? Or that a man was worth all that effort? God, wouldn't I love to have my own job and career and life instead of being stuck here looking after them and Dessie. Do they think that's so glamorous or what? But you might as well be idle as talking to them. They know it all.

'Well, if that's what you want to do, what can I do about it? It's not what I expected. You were in college for five years, and now as soon as you start earning, you're moving out. It's not what I would have done...but times change.'

'Yes they do. They change.'

'Where are you going to go?' she asked, with a gleam in her eye.

Nuala hadn't given the matter any thought. 'Well, I haven't found anywhere yet. Somewhere pretty close, I suppose. I don't know yet exactly where.'

Any old dive will do. Some kip of a bedsit on the South Circular not fit for a dog's home. Rats and filth. When she has a perfectly good home. She was always troublesome ever since she was a baby. Always very demanding, like, more so than the others really. Hungry and big and screaming. A fussy child if ever there was one.

'And when,' she asked grimly, 'are you moving out?'

Nuala hadn't thought about that either. Vague memories of flat-hunting stories flitted through her mind, and more concrete memories of Erik's mixed experiences in the bedsit world.

'Well, it'll take me a week or two to get organised.' She didn't want to put it on the long finger. Time and tide wait for no woman.

'Hm. What you should do is, get the *Evening Press* first thing, as soon as it comes out. Go down to Eason's and get it at one o'clock when it comes out. No good waiting till five o'clock in the evening, everything good will be gone by then. You be at the doors at four o'clock before the rest of them have got off work...'

Mollie got into her stride, giving advice, although she'd never hunted for a flat in her life. She couldn't resist the temptation, even though it was not in her own interest to give advice on this matter. A born busybody, Mollie was, taking a keen interest in everybody's affairs. She could have been a great organiser: a managing director or a reverend mother or the leader of a political party. She was wasted—she dimly sensed this herself—as a housewife.

Grateful for the change of mood, Nuala let her ramble on for a quarter of an hour, nodding and shaking her head for time to time, whatever was appropriate. Then she retired to her room and slept. It was the first night since Erik's departure from her life, that she slept soundly.

The impression of flat-hunting which Nuala had acquired from her mother, from Erik and from personal observation of lines of jaded-looking girls standing outside dingy hall-doors on the Rathmines Road was that it was a purgatorial experience. So she was taken aback to find a suitable place in less than half an hour. The reason for this seemed to be that she was searching at a time when few people were looking for what was available (nobody sane moves in early February) and that she had considerably more money at her disposal than most of those who were in the market for a student bedsitter. What she got was supposed to be a flat for two, consisting of one large room—the bedsit—and a minute kitchen. It wasn't the purpose-built apartment of her conservative dreams nor was it a picturesque Victorian suite overlooking a green or the sea, but it was more than adequate and initially seemed perfect: a large long room with white walls, an orange carpet and furniture made of chipboard. There were two divan beds, placed along the wall, and an electric artificial fire. The chimney breast was papered with turquoise wallpaper patterned in gold. Garish, but it worked and had a striking effect against the whiteness of the room.

The whole place was permeated by a stale sour smell, which could not be banished. It was only faintly unpleasant, however, and something you got used to and forgot about after a few minutes in the room. Still, it hit you every time you walked into that bedsit, a reminder of the years and years of frying that had been going on there. So many thousands of rashers and sausages, each adding its own minute odour to the deep ancient greasy pong permeating the furniture and the floor and the ceiling and the walls. But even this Nuala liked. It was as characteristic of the flat as the turquoise paper on the chimney breast or the beds draped in striped Indian blankets, which she purchased the minute she moved in. It was the smell of her first home, and as different as the smell of her parents' house as manure from roses. The typical aroma at 6 Exeter Place was of polish and pine disinfectant.

Give me grease.

Give me manure.

Give me mother earth.

Mollie did not discuss the move with Nuala after that first day. Nuala had feared that she had forgotten about it or hoped that by ignoring the issue it would disappear. But no. The day before she moved in, Mollie handed her a brown paper bag, which contained a china mug, an enormous china mug with a picture of a leaping hunter, in the pink, on its belly.

'You probably won't have a lot of delph in your new home,' she said drily.

'Thank you very much. It's lovely.'

Nuala was moved enough to tell Mollie the time of her departure.

'Sure it's well for the young ones nowadays.' Her voice had that mother of sorrows expression so common among parents of her generation. 'All they have to think about is how to enjoy themselves.'

Nuala had no comment to make on this.

'I suppose you'll need a lift over to the flat now, with all that stuff? I'd better ask Daddy to get out the car.'

So Mollie came round completely in the end. That was the way she was; she could accept any deviance from her children, given a few days to get accustomed to it. Nuala did not always appreciate her great adaptability. She knew of plenty of parents who were less tolerant of change: Roman fathers who laid down the law, did not allow their daughters out after ten, burned their mini-skirts. For them, with their staunch principles and strong personalities, she had a secret admiration. For her own parents' intuitive intelligence and flexibility, her esteem was scant.

CHAPTER ELEVEN

A few days after the move to the flat, Nuala bumped into Mary on the street. Not on Grafton Street, which was were she usually encountered people in this way, but on Camden Street, where she was shopping. The stalls had all kinds of delicious exotic samples of the fruit and vegetable kingdom for sale at a fraction of the supermarket price. Nuala was not entirely free of the obsession with bargain-hunting which was one of the most persistent traits of the particular sub-group of the working class to which she belonged and she probably never would be. Cheapness attracted her the way expensiveness attracts the rich and quality the middle classes. Camden Street had other things to offer besides good value, though: she wouldn't have bothered with it if it did not. It afforded a variety of pleasures to the eyes, ears, nose and throat (like the Eye and Ear Hospital, just around the corner). It was colourful, it was smelly, it was filled with fruity Dublin accents. Only fifty pence the kiwis, come on now, mam, I'll give you a dozen, only fifty pence a pound. The women would shout and wheedle, some of them almost grabbing your bag to put the stuff in before you'd even asked for it.

Nuala had shopped on this street with Mollie throughout her childhood. There had been—there still was—a fishmonger named Kattie on a small stall near the end of the street. She had a table laden with mackerel, herring, ray, cod and whiting, which she had wheeled up from the fishmarket in the early morning. Kattie—that was it, not Katy, which sounds glamorous and American—was as round as a barrel. Her body was wrapped in a winter coat of nondescript colour and her head in a little tight pink nylon headsquare. Her face, like most of the faces behind those stalls, was bright red and shiny; her eyes were anxious, coaxing. 'Only tenpence each the mackerdel!' she would cry, as soon as Mollie approached. 'Lovely mackerdel, only tenpence each!' And then she would hop out from behind the stall and start stuffing mackerel into Mollie's shopping bag, huge fat mackerel wrapped in newspaper.

'I only want half a dozen, Kattie. I can't use more than half a dozen.'

But she'd stuff them in, eight, ten, thirteen, sixteen. Twenty, if they were plentiful and hard to get rid of.

'There ye are now, mam, they're lovely and fresh today. Only a pound the lot, beautiful they are, fry them in oatmeal and eat them with spuds. Thanks very much, mam, God bless you.'

Now Nuala carefully avoided the end of the

street Kattie was on and stuck to the flower and
vegetable stalls, staffed by younger, less
assertive women. It was at one of these that she
met Mary, who was, just like her, carrying a
basketful of aubergine, pepper, lettuce, chillis,
and pineapple: the kind of thing Mollie never
bought.

'I hear you've moved out!' Mary dispensed
with any greeting and spoke what was on her
mind.

'Yeah. Someone had to make the break!'
retorted Nuala, with what she hoped was
good-humoured irony—a difficult note to
strike.

Mary was so cheerful that it succeeded. She
laughed her tinkly silvery laugh and threw
back her head. Her hair had been done: short
black waves caressed her cheeks. And she was
looking better than usual, even. Her face was a
shade plumper and her skin, naturally sallow
and verging on the lifeless, had become vibrant
and translucent without losing its delicate
brownish sheen. She was wearing a long
shapeless dress in a natural colour, of loosely
woven cotton, which she had tied at the waist
with a rope, of all things. It had a hood, the
dress, and looked decidedly cool and with-it. It
was the kind of dress Nuala would have loved
to own, but never had the guts to buy because
she wasn't revolutionary enought to spend a
small fortune on something that made such a
strong statement against capitalism. Mary's

dress reminded her of monks, of Indians, of
Jesus Mary and Joseph walking across the
desert. It reminded her of hippies and organic
farms and people living lovely artistic lives in
West Cork. She knew that such dresses were
hard to find in Dublin and over-priced.

'Come and have dinner with me!' Nuala
beamed. 'Come tomorrow night. You can have
a look at my flat then!'

To her surprise, Mary accepted.

'Bring John if you like.'

She would if she could. But sometimes he
had meetings and things in the evenings.

Nuala would expect him when she saw him,
she said cheerily, and then they parted, Nuala
walking up towards Portobello Bridge and
Rathmines and Mary in the opposite direction.
It struck Nuala for the first time that she did
not know where Mary lived. She had no idea
where she spent her days and nights and
neither did Dessie and Mollie. None of them
had dared to ask, or thought to ask. This
reluctance to check up on simple though crucial
facts, lest they upset some sort of delicately
balanced bucket of worms, was typical of them.
Oh how feeble they are! I'm feeble too. But
Nuala managed to push this unpleasant
thought out of mind. She'd find out tomorrow;
she'd get the address by some subtle ruse.
Think positive.

She was doing a lot of positive thinking
these days. Practically every five minutes she

had occasion to wag a mental finger at herself and recite the magic formula. It worked, sort of, most of the time. She was getting through. She still thought of Erik constantly but she did not cry more than once or twice a day. Sometimes she did not cry at all. She was finding ways of controlling the guerrilla attacks that still surprised her from time to time. When you are falling in love you've got to let down your defences. But when you are dragging yourself out of it you've got to build them up again. She was beginning to understand that much, although she did not yet understand that you have to be able to change your tack fairly regularly if you want to live an interesting and fulfilled life as a single woman. Even though she had done it once before, she imagined that this was the last time. She believed that if she got those fences up again they would stay up, and that that was what growing to maturity meant.

She felt triumphant when she thought of Erik. He believed she was such a weakling. How surprised he would be to find out about the flat! (She had no doubt that he would find out, and very soon. The grapevine would quickly take care of that.) Her flat, her home! And such an improvement on any of the dives he'd ever had. She'd made every effort to make it cosy, comfortable, to give it soul. Often she felt that the cool hippy flower-power confidence and happiness that, although much desired, had eluded her so far, was just around the corner, like a slim, fluffy, fast, giddy, happy rabbit, hopping and dancing, staring with wide laughing eyes, waiting to be caught. Not around the corner, right in front of her, skipping and tripping and smiling and winking. All she would have to do, when the moment was ripe, was put out her hand and grab him, and then she would have it, have it, have it for ever more. The gift of happiness. The gift of hippiness. The gift of peacefulness

The scheme would be aided by a suitable setting and appropriate tools: so the flat was hung with posters of abstract pictures in muted pastels, it had cheesecloth curtains and trailing bottle green plants. There were stripy Indian things on the bed and the floor, and sticks of incense in hand-thrown jars burning at all hours of the day and night on the chipboard chest of drawers. In front of the fireplace was a large fan-like object, said to come from Japan, and on the mantelpiece a fat golden Buddha, acquired in the Indian shop on Old Camden Street. She would have liked a budgie or a finch in a wooden cage, but thought better of it. Birds require care, and besides she really felt it cruel to imprison them. A parrot, a big colourful bossy parrot, living on a perch over rhe bed, free to come and go within the limits of the bedsitter, might have been the answer. But perhaps parrots were a bit eccentric, a bit Victorian, a bit conservative. Besides, they most certainly were outrageously expensive.

So she forgot the birds. But the rest of her effects pleased her, and, when she spent evenings alone in her little nest, dressed in a black fringed skirt and a white smock with gold embroidery on it, and Indian slippers of crimson and black and gold with turned-up toes, sipping dark red wine and listening to her LPs, she felt almost...almost...almost happy.

But never quite so. There was still something there, dragging her away from bliss. Dragging her down, like the sinking feeling of the womb before a period, drowning her hope. There was that thing, that terrible unknown, for all she knew unknowable, magnet, that ghastly gravity, pulling, pulling.

Even when she was fully engaged in some enjoyable activity, she was never completely unselfconscious. Every so often she withdrew, lost concentration and observed herself at work. Even when she was cooking. She was a good cook, although she'd never had any formal instruction and little practice apart from the meals she'd created for Erik in Erik's flat. Mollie, who had taught Mary and Nuala to help with the washing-up and the cleaning when they were aged about four, had been such a keen cook herself that she'd never asked them to lend a hand with it. It didn't matter. Nuala, who had been on a semi-starvation diet since she was seventeen, suddenly discovered the joy of cooking. It was such fun to come home from work and mix things together. Tasty casseroles, piquant pastas, succulent soups appeared every evening in her kitchen. She was getting quite pudgy.

For Mary and John she made moussaka, with a green salad. For dessert there would be ice-cream for her and Mary and cheese for John. She had read in a book called *Cooking in a Bedsitter*—which was full of horrible ideas for desserts of crumbled biscuits and jam, and dinners of jambalaya—that men disliked sweet things and appreciated cheese. All guests, the book said, would appreciate food of the freshest and best quality. Creamy new butter, crispy bread. If the hostess took care of these small things, any lack of variety or exoticism would be overlooked. The party would succeed. When you go to the country to visit your parents at the weekend bring home a basketful of garden produce and remember always, always, put on your make-up before the guests arrive. That way they'll think your sparkling green eyelids are natural.

Mary came alone. So much for the cheese. (Nuala had it on bread, no longer fresh and crusty, for lunch next day.) John had had a meeting after all. On a Sunday?

'He was really apologetic. He'd love to meet you.' Mary deposited a bottle of wine on the table. 'I'll open this now, can I? It's Rioja. It's supposed to breathe for ages.'

'That's too bad,' said Nuala, handing her the

corkscrew. I could have guessed he wouldn't show up. Afraid to show his ugly face.

'Is Erik coming?' Mary was struggling with the cork, which seemed to have been wedged in much too firmly. Her face was red with effort, almost the colour of her dress—puce velvet. Where did she get all the gear? Never the same garment twice nowadays, on her of the jeans and Shetland sweaters.

'No, he's not,' said Nuala shortly. She was about to say that he was at a meeting too. But she was not in the habit of lying, to Mary or anyone else. Even the social art of the white lie she had not managed to learn. So she continued: 'We've broken it off, actually.'

'Oh!' Mary waved the cork triumphantly aloft. 'Oh dear. That surprises me, I must say.'

Nuala was taken aback. Did this mean that it wasn't obvious to everyone in the world that she was not good enough for Erik and that he would eventually have to leave her?

'Why?'

'Well,' Mary replied, in flat earnest tone, 'I just thought you and Erik were one of those couples that was bound to last forever. You seemed so well suited, somehow.'

'Hmm.'

Nuala felt upset, for a minute, thinking that she had made yet another mistake. If she'd had faith in the relationship maybe it would have lasted. Then she felt warm and gratified, enlarged by this praise, this linking of her to

Erik.

Oh Erik. Erik.

'Oh yes,' went on Mary, as Nuala placed a Pyrex dish upon the table, on a nice straw mat. The dish itself was supposed to be white, with red daisies on it, but it had been burned a ripe brown colour from years of burning in the bedsit oven. Mary took the serving spoon and helped herself to some of the gooey stuff. 'Oh yes, I'd imagined you'd get married soon.'

'Oh no!' Nuala suddenly learned about white lies. 'Marriage is the last thing I want.' The words emerged thickly, coated with cheese sauce and bits of mince meat, so that their raw untruthful edge was blunted.

'Are you sure?' Mary cocked her head on one side and waved her fork in the air, waggishly.

'Yes. Of course I am. Why shouldn't I be?'

'Oh, I don't know.' She stared at the poster opposite her, and allowed tomato sauce to drip from her fork on to the table. 'It's just that everyone I know wants to, you know. All the women, that is…nearly all.' She drank some wine. 'I mean, obviously they don't go around shouting about it all the time, and actually quite a few of them pretend not to care. But they do. I know it. They're sort of anxious about it all the time, do you know what I mean? I'd begun to think it must be the result of some sort of conditioning. You know, an inescapable thing, the wish to marry, for people

175

brought up like us. Brought up to think along certain lines.'

She had another drink and Nuala poured some more wine. The bottle was nearly empty. They'd have to start on the Rioja soon, and it had only been breathing for half an hour. Lucky John hadn't come.

'Of course,' she mused, sipping again, 'it might be my age. I am older than you.'

'Yes,' said Nuala eagerly. 'Do you mean you're conditioned to start wanting to get married when you're twenty-three or something, but not before?'

'It sounds ridiculous, doesn't it, put like that? But yes, I do think so. I think we set watersheds for ourselves, consciously or unconsciously. We say: I'll get married when I'm twenty-five, or twenty-six, or something. And then if that age passes and we're not married we begin to worry.'

Twenty-two was my age. And Erik the man. I'm worried.

'I don't think it sounds ridiculous.' Nuala passed her the salad. 'But I'm not at my watershed, not yet. There are so many things I want to do first. Anyway, most of the marriages I hear about start for only one reason.'

'Oh that!' Mary laughed her silvery good-humoured laugh, which always made Nuala feel a bit inferior: too grave, too lugubrious. 'Well, what can you expect in a place where men don't really ever want to get married, and women do?'

'Oh, that's not true, is it? I know men who want to get married.'

Sean, for instance. And that guy Jean's engaged to. What'shisname. And I know at least two others who would have married me if I'd let them. Two, or three, or maybe four. Of course they were not men like Erik. Erik wasn't interested in marriage. But he wasn't Irish, for heaven's sake. It obviously was unfair to blame Irishmen for being the unmarrying type.

'There are exceptions to every rule,' Mary said with a smile. 'The ones who are too boring or too young or too old or too ugly or too crazy, usually. And the ones who never have a job and the ones who never have a bath. They like getting married."

'Oh no. There are nice men who marry, too.'

'Nice. But not the kind of men you or I want to marry. Right?'

This sounded true. 'Nice men are not attractive.' As a statement, it had a ring of authenticity to it.

'Isn't that our problem? We go for the wrong type. It's not their fault, is it?'

'I don't think we go for the wrong type. Why should we? Why should we both, and half the women we know, all our friends, go for the wrong type? What we go for is our own type, men who are like us, the male counterpart of ourselves. Naturally we go for them. And they don't want to get married.'

'You mean they don't want to marry us?'

'Yes. Or anyone, and especially not at the time we want it. They'll want it earlier, or later, but never at the same time. It's not because there's anything wrong with us, though. It's because there's something wrong with them.'

'What?'

'They can't stand women who have ideas of their own. They have to rule the roost in the relationship. Also they usually aren't in love with us at the same time that we're in love with them. They fall for us at the beginning, and we let them. By the time we've fallen for them they've moved on to another phase. Which could be called the phase of affectionate indifference.'

'Mm. So why do we love them?'

'They're persistent. And they're attractive. And we're made the way we're made or conditioned the way we're conditioned.'

'What is it they've got, that nice men haven't?'

'A BA in history, usually, I think. That sort of thing. I mean, so-called cultured Irishmen are afraid of so-called cultured Irish women. I've noticed that more and more of late.'

'Have you really?'

'Yes. Its not just that they don't want to marry them—and they do marry in the end, most of them. They capitulate in the end and give up their ideal. They marry someone whom they think is safe and pretty enough. But they never accept women was equals, you know, not as equally intelligent. Just listen to a crowd of historians or writers or critics, male ones, talking among themselves!'

'I never have.'

'Well, do sometime, just do. Or read what they write when they're being chatty in print. Informal commentaries after someone famous, one of them, has died or something. It's all he and him and the scholar or writer or whatever as a man...like when they're drunk, drunk and serious now that someone's dropped dead, they forget that women exist. As far as that kind of man is concerned, women hardly exist, except as sexual objects. You catch them with their hair down at a party or a funeral, among the lads, and you'll soon see what I mean.'

'Have you been to any funerals lately?'

Mary frowned.

'No.'

'I don't mean to be facetious... it's just such an unusual image...men at a funeral.'

'I thought you'd know what I mean.'

'Well, I do, probably. But it's all so complicated isn't it? I mean, I know its true, what you say. They're scared of women, especially the kind of men we like, and they despise us especially because...'

'Because they see us as incompetent competitors, probably. They half-fear us and half-despise us. Mainly they believe we're stupid, but sometimes they wonder, just a little.

179

They have faint uneasy misgivings…maybe they're stupid, after all. Which is, in my opinion, the case. They are emotionally and socially stupid. They are out of touch with their instincts. And instinct and intelligence are very closely linked."

Funny attitude in someone whose in the middle of a passionate affair, anticipating marriage. Mary's going slightly gaga at last. Or has she come under some baleful influence, has she been trucking with those women's libbers?

'I suppose so. But we still like them, we love them, don't we? There's something about them that we love.'

I want to weep, I want to scream. Erik Erik Erik come back all is forgiven I love you more than ever. I really love you more than Vogue does. I know I do.

'I think that view is getting outdated, to tell you the truth. I mean, it may be like that for me or you, but it won't be for younger women. They'll feel differently about these questions, I think.'

'You seem to feel differently about them yourself, don't you? Perhaps you shouldn't get married after all.'

Mary laughed a lot, and hysterically. She became quite red in the face again, redder than her dress this time, as red as the wine. Nuala was afraid she might choke. 'Perhaps you're right, Nuala. I think you've hit the nail on the head. But there's something else. We'd better drink to it before all this shit is gone. I'm pregnant! Pregnant, just like all the rest of them! So of course I'll be getting married.'

She patted her velvet stomach and raised her glass.

CHAPTER TWELVE

After the parting from Nuala, Erik had felt despondent and guilty. Trust her to make him feel like that! She was nothing if not negative, always pouring cold water over everything. In an attempt to purge these unpleasant feelings, he plunged, not into the high life that Nuala assumed he must be living, but into work. It was in any case essential that he do something about his thesis very quickly. He had done practically no work for three months, what with one thing and another. His bloody mother! Forget her, forget her!

Every day for a month found him in the library, from early morning until the place closed at nine o clock. He was writing his thesis, not just doing research, making notes or drawing up plans, all of which he had been at sporadically for two years, but actually writing it, page by page, chapter by chapter, in a form close to that which it would finally take. He had not, really, believed that it would be possible, that he had what it took to fill pages with text, to keep filling them until something that could be described as a book would appear. It had seemed too amazing a task, too great a creative effort, from the abstract perspective of someone reading articles and taking notes. The reality was so much more workaday and practical, so unmiraculous, that it stunned him. Gratified him too. Hell, it was easy! Once you got started, once you got into it, it happened.

But was it good?

This question did not worry Erik initially. He did not, at first, really care whether it was good or not. That it was simply there, extant, Chapter One and Chapter Two and Chapter Three, was sufficiently satisfactory. Only when three chapters, about a hundred pages, had been completed, did he begin to ponder this problem. At that stage, in the new mood of pragmatism which he was enjoying, he simply took the chapters, brought them to his supervisor, and asked for an opinion. This was naturally not immediately forthcoming, and in the interval of waiting he took what anyone would have considered a well-earned rest.

The thought of a booze-up with Binjy occurred to him as a possible way to let off steam. But on consideration he decided against it. Decadence had lost its appeal, somehow. All that hard slogging was turning him into a puritan of sorts. Or was it the residue of the visit to Copenhagen, the memory of his mother, which he was busily suppressing? Go away mother. (Kirsten wrote, once a week, as usual, often mentioning Elsa *en passant* as if it were the most natural thing in the world. He had stopped reading the letters. A childish ploy, he knew, but knowing it did not help him to overcome his anxiety, or to find a more sophisticated technique for coping with it.)

It was important, this he did know, to find some intensive activity to replace the frenetic writing which he had been doing for a month, for five weeks. Time without work yawned like a trap. He did not know where he would land if he were not careful. Above all, he must not yield to the temptation, ever present, to return to Nuala. Old habits die hard. He was used to her; she was, in her rough difficult way, a familiar, a comfort. He must not, for her sake as well as for his own—thus he argued—give in. He must find something to do.

He could have carried on working, of course. The fact that Dr Hennessy had three chapters did not mean that he could not continue to write more. But he needed an alternative, for a week.

Vogue.

He had not, contrary to Nuala's suspicions, seen Vogue since Christmas: the bottle of perfume he had bought for Nuala, in anticipation of her birthday, which was in March. He had assumed that they would still be friends, always be friends, even though at Christmas he had known that he did not, for the moment, want to continue the relationship at a deeper level. He had hardly given a moment's thought to Vogue since the time he had last met her in O'Neill's pub. He was, however, as Nuala suspected, attracted to her, although not very much. And he was also in possession of her telephone number. So, he rang her up and invited her to dinner, and she accepted.

They went to an Italian restaurant on Leeson Street, where Erik had not been before but which Vogue had frequented with her father. The Pygmalion. There were pictures of George Bernard Shaw and of Greek statues on the walls, as well as a reproduction of Van Gogh's 'Sunflowers', which was just then becoming *de rigueur* in all fashionable restaurants. It was a small place, intimate in atmosphere, dealing in pastas, of course, and as an alternative, conservative Irish cuisine. Porksteak and chicken and roast potatoes and so on. The decor was surprisingly—considering that Vogue's father used the place—plain: plain painted walls, no tablecloths, just straw mats.

'They used to have hemp table mats!' Vogue giggled. 'I smoked one of them once; it was great!' She laughed and was happy. In her element, here as in so many places. Erik appreciated her giddiness, her positive outlook. She was small, cheerful, carefree. And pretty, especially tonight, dressed up in a mushroom blouse and black velvet harem pants, with several strings of tiny multicoloured plastic beads strung around her neck. She exuded confidence, and a certain kind of joy: her pleasure in being herself. She did not look at the other diners; they, or their clothes, or their habits, or their food, were of no apparent interest to her. Totally self-absorbed, self-sufficient, as she was.

They ate *prosciutto* and tomatoes, ravioli with cream and spinach, a special creamy cheesecake. No wine. Vogue was teetotalling tonight, and even this Erik found very satisfactory. I hate wine, really, he told her, seriously, and he meant it, although he hadn't realised it until now. Wine makes me feel sick. Beer is much better.

You should always drink beer in North Atlantic regions, Vogue informed him. Received wisdom, from her father. This is the beer butter oats belt. The south is the wine olives wheat belt. Of course we're in that belt, so to speak, in this restaurant, but it doesn't matter. The wheat seems to travel better than the wine.

They talked about Vogue's school and the subjects she was doing in the Leaving and about Erik's thesis and its progress and about Vogue's father. And not about Nuala or Erik's mother or Copenhagen except as a tourist resort, which was how Vogue knew it. Erik told her about a murder which had been committed in the harbour district, a district she knew on account of the Little Mermaid, just a year previously. A Turkish woman had been stabbed to death by her brother-in-law, aged eighteen, because she had dared to divorce his brother. The family honour had to be defended. He had acted on his father's instructions. His father had written from Turkey: 'Buy a knife and murder Ayse.' And he had done so. And was immediately caught and imprisoned, where he had languished for a year, awaiting torture which the authorities did not provide, of course. So in the end he imagined it himself, imagined he was bound by an iron ring and could not breathe. And went mad.

All in all, a pleasant evening. Vogue did not share the bill, which was higher than Erik had anticipated, and this had a mildly disgruntling effect on him. But on the whole he was happy with the experiment, and resolved to repeat it in the near future at a restaurant of his own choice.

CHAPTER THIRTEEN

Mary was pregnant. She was manifesting tendencies to be a man-hater. Nevertheless she was going to marry a man, a married man, John Smyth, twenty years her senior, as soon as he could obtain a divorce, which might not be for several years, which might be never.

She was abandoning her thesis, her ambitions, her career.

'It's no good going on,' she said. 'I'm just not good enough. I'm not in the same league as, say, John. Let's be realistic, even if I did manage to finish the thing, it probably wouldn't pass. It would never get published. John says it's not worth pursuing: with the baby, we'll have enough on our plates. After all, I can't do everything!'

Nuala was more shocked by Mary's decision to abandon her thesis than by her pregnancy or her decision to marry John Smyth. Although Mary's reasoning seemed logical enough—how could she do everything?—Nuala found it hard to accept. She sensed, dolefully, genetic weakness, in this casual, lazy capitulation, this easy succumbing to circumstance. The heart ruling the head. It was a family characteristic among the Byrnes, a baleful gift handed on from generation to generation. Pass the poisoned parcel. They lacked confidence, the Byrnes. They lacked drive. They lacked, above all, good sound sense. Mollie had told her, more than once, of the scholarship she had won to a boarding school in Meath when she had finished the primary stage of her schooling. She'd been first in her class; the teacher had been most encouraging. But did she go? No. She stayed in Dublin and worked in a shop. She'd worked in a shop for ten years cutting bacon and slicing cheese, and then she'd married Dessie. She could have been a civil servant or a schoolteacher or a nurse. Or—this was not likely—a doctor or a solicitor or a writer. But she became none of these things because she couldn't bear to leave her mother and father. Even for school terms in County Meath.

The Byrnes are like that. They're fools. They never get on.

It's in the blood. Look what I did just seven or eight months ago, and where is he now?

Mary's defeatism, as it seemed to her, fixed Nuala in her determination to get out of the office and to find a meaningful career, an alternative to the academic life she had now left behind her. The method she employed in achieving this goal was not, perhaps, the best. She did not, in fact, take the matter into her own hands, but trusted to contingency: the

Byrnes were gamblers, Dessie went to the dogs at Shelbourne Park every Monday. What Nuala did was examine the newspapers every Friday, when the advertisements for jobs appeared, and apply for anything that looked faintly promising. Teaching positions, for which she was not qualified, were her first choice. She met with a few pleasant interviews but not with any concrete results. Her interview for the Diplomatic Service, which she thought would be interesting on account of the foreign lands and the glamour, was less enjoyable, since it concerned current affairs about which she knew nothing at all. Like the teacher interviews, it led to nought. Even her longest shot, an application for a training course in electronics, drew a blank. It had a positive side-effect, in that she met some odd characters through it, notably a woman with the unlikely name of Myrtle Muggy, who had been trying for a year to get a job, any kind of job, and who kept telling Nuala and the other women doing the aptitude tests how lucky they were.

'Yeah, I've tried everything, everything bar housework and childminding. I'll do anything else. Though mind you it's not bad, is it? It's not taxed, is it? By the time you pay tax and all you don't have much left, do you?'

Myrtle was English. That's why she talked like that. Also she was about to have her period, which put her at a disadvantage, she told Nuala.

'They should take it into account, shouldn't they, though? I mean to say, you're not yourself on your off-days, are you? You can't perform, yeah. When I woke this morning and saw it I said, Cor blimey, I might have known, just your luck, Myrtle, it is, isn't it? Couldn't wait another day, had to be today. No wonder they call it the curse is what I say. Yeah.'

Nuala did not get a place on the electronics course. But she wrote a short and, she hoped, comic report of the aptitude tests, including a graphic account of Myrtle, and sent it to a new magazine called *In Dublin*. To her gratification they published it, and sent her five pounds. She began to think about journalism. Yeah, I've always wanted to be a journalist, yeah. Come to think of it. I've tried everything, this could be my last shot. Yeah.

Yeah. Cor blimey. Thank you, Myrtle, thanks a lot. May you have a warm place on the assembly line, if you get a warm place on the course first, in spite of menstrual obstacles. You're right, of course, Myrtle, and why don't I write a bit about menstruation, it's a sure-fire winner. If I can get any paper brave enough to publish it.

The night after the publication of her article, Nuala went out to Fairfield, to the lecture Jean had told her about. It was a last-minute decision, inspired less by interest in the topic than by a mercenary suspician that there might be good copy in it. How much more exciting life was, now that there was a possibility of writing about everything that cropped up. It added a new dimension to experience: no longer was it just itself, a sort of textureless unrealisable present which would soon become a forgotten unrealised past. Now it was raw material, shapeless in itself, perhaps, but pregnant with possibilities. Comedy, tragedy, farce, drama: all emerged from this pale amorphous thing called life, that thing which everyone had, which everyone experienced, but, for the most part, only half-consciously. All you had to do to make readable copy out of it was pull it into shape. A tug here, a tuck there. A little emphasis on the more startling points. Hey presto. You'd something quite different. It was like cooking dirty raw vegetables and hard stringy cheese and chunks of messy meat and ending up with a cordon bleu dish—or some sort of dish—which bore little resemblance to its raw ingredients, although it was no more than the sum of those ingredients, plus some heat.

Ah yes! Everything was changing as the proverbs, the horoscopes, the agony aunties promised. Leave them alone and they'll come home, wagging, wagging, wagging.

She strode along, from Leinster Road down to Ranelagh and on out through Clonskeagh. A long walk, longer than she had taken in months. But her new hobby, as well as the new season, energised her. Spring had come; it had suddenly, overnight, arrived, or perhaps it is truer to say that it had arrived on this very evening, as she was coming out her hall door into the long, damp green garden of the lodging house. Because then, for the first time this year, she sensed the sharp tangy air, the pulsating earthiness, the push and shove and striving in the atmosphere, that means spring. It was no surprise to see small girls playing beds on one of the lanes, hopping from square to square, kicking a polish tin energetically. The hop had come back to life, and that is a good thing, if you are twenty-two and almost recovered from a love affair and embarking on a new enthusiasm, which, for the moment, is a good substitute for love itself.

How she enjoyed it, that first long walk on that first spring evening! She enjoyed the pale lingering light, the deep soft green of the reviving grass, the pale green frills of the earlier trees. She enjoyed the heavy shower of rain that came through the sunshine; she was wearing a raincoat, because it had been showery all day. And after the rain, she enjoyed to the point of ecstasy the heavenly smell which arose from the gardens. She was in Clonskeagh at this point, passing suburban houses with neat well tended lawns in front, and she supposed the scent, almost unnnaturally rich, which she had previously experienced only as emanating from a cut-glass bottle of Dior perfume, belonging to

Mary, must derive from some flower or other. But all she could see were daffodils, an early tulip or two, some sprays of forsythia. The aroma seemed to arise from the ground itself, extracted from the clay by the cleansing shower. 'When that Aprille, with his shoures sote/The droghte of March hath perced to the rote'. The opening lines of *The Canterbury Tales* popped into her head. She had not really understood exactly what he was talking about when he mentioned 'showers sweet'. But now she did know, precisely, with her nose, and the sudden discovery, totally private and totally useless to anyone else, pleased her very much.

Borne along by her satisfaction, she reached Fairfield in time for the lecture. She felt tired, however, since it had been a walk of four miles, uphill, and since she had moved at high speed. She went into one of the underground cloakrooms to freshen up, and when she emerged, like a mole, and darted into the lecture theatre, it was already half-full and the speaker was in the process of being introduced.

Nuala found a seat at the back. After a minute she spotted Jean, down near the podium. Jean turned, scanned the tiers of faces, and finally waved exuberantly in Nuala's direction. Nuala waved discreetly back. Jean's eyes did not meet hers, however, but those of a woman sitting directly in front of her, who was, with exuberance equal to Jean's, blowing a kiss at the latter. Nuala felt faintly stunned, and her spring-feeling diminished in her veins. Trust that Jean!

A woman with fuzzy blond hair and bright round eyes, dressed all in purple, was introducing the speaker. Lane, she was telling the audience, had written ten books, held fifteen different positions in universities and other prestigious institutions and sat on innumerable committees and so on. It sounded like a very busy life, not what Nuala would have considered an alternative lifestyle at all. Nor did Lane match the standard image of the common or garden alternative liver: she did not have long hair, a long skirt, a Tolstoy shirt. She did not look like a person who had ever milked an organically fed goat, made cottage cheese or woven a length of nubbly tweed. Indeed she did not look as if she had ever boiled an egg, free-range or battery. What she looked like was a career woman. Her careful coiffure, her neat make-up meant business. Her stylish, subdued, expensive clothes proclaimed it. She might have been a well-known television personality, a popular politician, director of a travel agency or a public relations outfit. Someone highly competitive, committed, and successful. And that is exactly what she was.

Well, it was an alternative, in a way, to the sort of lives most people live, which, in Dublin at that time, as far as Nuala had noticed, were closer to the simple mediocrity of the subsistence farm than you might imagine, if you were an American urbanite like Lane. It was an alternative to the slow humdrum life of the PAYE worker, to their near-poverty, their difficult-to-maintain respectability. A welcome alternative, too, no doubt, the kind that sent many scuttling off to American or London. But Nuala and the others had not come out to Fairfield on the first day of spring to hear about visas and work permits.

What they heard about was marriage. There was no getting away from this subject. Lane was talking about alternatives to that, nothing else. As if marriage or non-marriage were the whole of life, as if farms and pet lambs had nothing to do with it. The main choice in life was not that between the rat-race and the hen-run, but between being married or not being married.

Lane was not herself married. Not at the moment. But, being American, she had been, in the past. When she was twenty, and about to graduate from college, she'd married, like most of her classmates. We just couldn't wait! she laughed. It was the thing to do! And then she'd been divorced, just two years after the wedding. It had been one of those silly mistakes kids make! Since then, she'd had many affairs, very warm and loving relationships with men and women, which had been, in their time, enormously satisfying and rewarding. But—and this was the nub of it— her periods of celibacy ('Believe me, it's possible!')—were also rewarding. They had been times of great wonder, great creativity, during which the world had been remade for her. 'Believe me, it's possible!' The audience sniggered dutifully.

All the marital alternatives to actual marriage with children were mentioned, analysed and judged. The lecture concluded that, although there were disadvantages attaching to every lifestyle, the very worst, the bottom of the pit, as far as women were concerned, was marriage with children. The victims of that kind of relationship were, inevitably, the wives and mothers. They gave all, received least, suffered. Marriage without children or no marriage at all were vastly preferable. Unmarried motherhood was not mentioned, but the implication was that it could be preferable to married maternity.

The talk lasted for about half an hour, which passed on winged feet because Lane's style was vigorous and gripping. She bounced, she laughed, she stressed, she seduced, as television personalities do. She was never angry or ironic, as feminists can be. She was never dull, as academics frequently are. She held the large audience spellbound. Her ideas, although they were thin enough, had the fascination of novelty, in that place and at that time. Lane was opening a gateway; she was pecking away a chink in some Berlin wall that divided expectation from reality.

While the woman in purple thanked Lane in purple prose, Nuala surveyed the gathering. Most of it consisted of a type of Dublin womanhood with which she was all too unfamiliar. Women in accurately faded jeans and loose black sweaters, with faces topped by mops of fuzzy hair, who belonged to the artistic community or the feminist community or to some other desirable, trendy, closed shop. (Clothes shop was nearer the mark: Nuala and her contemporaries were at the stage when appearances and promise meant everything, because nobody was old enough to have proved anything one way or the other as yet.) These cool suave creatures, seeming confident in their belonging, were the kind of women you could expect to see at any lecture or event of a feminist or artistic or political nature. They belonged, indisputably, in the milieu of this theatre, with Lane. It was them she addressed, it was them she spoke of, because they were part of a community which bridged nations and which was as American as it was Irish. Brave, rebellious, classless, liminal. Artists, academics, free-lance journalists. So they appeared to be. Young, untried, and brimming over with confidence and optimism, they looked like winners to Nuala.

And the other half of the audience looked like losers, to her young and critical eye. Librarians and secretaries and women from administration, instantly recognisable by the cut of their clothes and hair and shoes. Working women, neat and clean and politely subdued, from the crowns of their unostentatious coiffures to their little demi-heels. She summed them up as feminine but not sexy, cheerful but not flamboyant, well-dressed but not trendy. Classic styles. Classic faces. Classic personalities.

These were real women, not naïve girls whose revolutionary ideas and lofty ambitions would dissolve, all too soon, in the murky realities of anti-feminism and unemployment, or disappear in suburban semis. But Nuala did not know it, and Lane did not recognise it. Her remarks about marriage and its terrible disadvantages could not have been addressed to them. They were, hardly any of them, married, because hardly any working women were married, still less had children. And what married woman with children comes to a lecture at seven o'clock on a Tuesday evening? Lane suffered jet-lag, in more ways than one.

When the purple-clad woman, who was an academic, therefore, to Nuala's eye, a liminal, special creature, had finished her remarks, and the topic was thrown to the floor for discussion, these polite sensible women did not say anything. They nodded, they smiled, they shook their heads from time to time, but they did not open their mouths and speak. The women who carried on the discussion were the young female academics, of whom their were three, a few of the fuzzy black sweater brigade, the purple-clad woman and Lane.

They were professional disputants, with years of experience behind them, and the discussion was lively, as the paper had been lively. But, whereas the paper had concerned itself with a variety of alternatives to marriage, the discussion focused on one point only: why people want to marry at all. For comfort, security, children, escape from loneliness: these were some of the reasons adduced. But no solution was arrived at. Still, it was interesting, from Nuala's perspective, the perspective of a woman who had just a few days earlier decided that she did not, after all, want to marry, to hear the institution she had wanted for so long to belong to denigrated so vehemently, scorned and derided. It was very uplifting.

What was more interesting, if a trifle disconcerting, was the general implication of the speakers that marriage was there for the asking. To hear the confident, brash young women talking, you would imagine that all women were constantly besieged by proposals from eligible men. You would imagine that they spent their time wondering who they should date next, who they should drop. You would imagine that they were all Scarlett O'Hara.

In Dublin, Scarlett O'Hara would have had a rough time, at least after her twenty-third birthday or so.

Nuala could see a face she recognised—

apart from Jean's, which she could not see anyway—at the opposite side of the theatre. It was a small, pretty face, fortyish, and it belonged to a woman in Rathmines who worked in the library. Her name was Ann and she had been living with her aunt all her life. Nuala doubted if she'd ever had a proposal. She wondered it she'd ever had a date. Not because she was unattractive. In fact she was beautiful: she had long blond hair, tied back (of course) in a sort of chaste pony tail. She had a perfect face, a perfect figure, and her clothes were appealing. In personality she was very affable. Therein, perhaps, lay the problem. She was simply too nice. Too virtuous to survive in Dublin. Not a schemer or manipulator, she believed what she had been told about patience, discretion, men. She was waiting. Waiting. In a place like this, you could not afford to wait, if you were a woman. Because all the men were waiting too.

For Ann, as for fifty per cent of the women at the lecture, the question of marrying or not marrying was entirely academic. So Nuala judged, with the cruelty of youth. Judged not quite correctly (Ann had dated heaps of men and had had three proposals) but not altogether inaccurately either. There is in every society a middle group of ladies—parsons' daughters, teachers' daughters, women like Jane Austen, or the Brontë sisters—whose expectations are higher than their qualifications, in the line of parentage, money and looks. In Dublin, this group seemed to be exceptionally large even in the 1970s, a period when you would not have expected the values of Jane Austen's England to be very prevalent anywhere.

Lane did not know about this fascinating aspect of life in Ireland. If she had done, she would have written a new article, or even a series of articles or a book, about it. But she didn't, and she would not find out, because the secretaries would be the last the let her know. Whatever secrets they had, they were keeping them tucked in behind their slim waists and slightly pursed, lipsticked mouths.

When the meeting was finished, most people filed out, and some groups gathered in the concourse outside the theatre. Nuala lingered there hopefully and eventually Jean arrived.

'Hi there!' She did not look Nuala in the eye, and her voice was faintly strained. 'Hi there! Glad you managed to get here!'

Bitch.

'Hello Jean.'

'Well, do you know Aileen?'

The purple one.

'Listen, we're just going to the bar for a drink with Lane. Would you like to come?'

'Yes, thank you.'

'I just have to go up to the English department first, with Aileen, to collect something…Listen, why don't you wait here?

We'll be back in two flicks of a lamb's tail.'

Mmm.

While she was waiting, Nuala examined a large notice board outside the chaplain's office, which happened to be in the vicinity. It advertised, among church and musical events, some scholarhips. A number of European countries—Austria, Germany, Norway, Sweden, Denmark, Finland—invited applications from Irish post-graduates. Nuala scanned the advertisements with interest: nobody had ever told her that such possibilities existed. The closing dates for most of the places were gone. The only two that were still available were Denmark and Finland. Denmark was out, for now and forever. Finland? Finland wanted an Irish student who would learn Finnish and take a course in comparative literature. The scholarship was for one year initially, with the possibility of an extension.

Finland. What do I know about Finland? Helskinki is the capital. There's a composer called Sibelius from there, and they design things. Glasses, maybe. Then they have saunas, lakes, and snow.

Literature? Nuala had never heard of even one Finnish writer. But she made a note of the address and the closing date, and thought that she probably would have a bash at it anyway. Maybe journalism wasn't such a great idea after all. Literature had been her first love.

CHAPTER FOURTEEN

Erik's thesis was returned to him, with encouraging comments, and he began to write with renewed vigour. He forgot to ring Vogue again, and, as he became increasingly absorbed in his work, he forgot that he had decided that he would do so. Nuala remained at the back of his mind, a lingering pinprick : he did not feel, as she assumed, that he had banished her completely from his life and heart. Occasionally he worried about her and regretted that they had moved on to different wavelengths. Sometimes he missed her and wished that she would move back into his life again. But he didn't miss her enough to do anything about it. If chance brought about a reunion, he would have accepted this as a gift of fortune, but he was wary of taking any initiative in this matter himself. He did not analyse his reasoning or feelings. It was easier to ignore them.

Most of the time ignoring them was very easy indeed, since his work was so utterly absorbing. The most significant thing in the world, by far, was 'The Friar's Tale'. That 'interesting' story, as those who did not frankly refer to it as 'not my favourite tale' tended to dub it, was now the only thorn in Erik's head, and what a glorious, lambent, stimulating problem it was. One of a crown of glorious, glittering, inspiring prickles, the star among its large circle of analogues. Could any question be more thorny than the one he asked constantly, but was well in the way of answering: 'What is the source of this poem?' He imagined, implicitly, a world waiting with bated breath for the results of his research. 'At last, at last!' the people would cry. 'At last someone had found the solution ! Our thirst for knowledge is quenched—momentarily at least. Bravo, Erik!'

Time itself, although undoubtedly his ally in the matter of forgetting Nuala, no longer held any of its usual meaning for him. He had simply lost track of it. The urbane routines which had sustained him through the initial, less inspired, stages of his work were gradually abandoned. No longer did he lunch regularly at one. Indeed he frequently did not lunch at all. Sleep he took when he felt like it. Sometimes this might be at nine o'clock in the evening, sometimes at three in the morning. As time—to which he was so gloriously indifferent—went on, he slept less and less, and ate at the typewriter, grabbing a sandwich or a chunk of unbuttered bread from his flatlet kitchenette, gulping down a bottle or two of milk when, out of the blue, he felt thirsty. He was growing thin and very pale, and also, to save time, a beard. Anybody who saw him shuddered and thought: he looks wretched. But few people did see him—nobody, really, apart from Mrs Flynn, the flabby woman in the newsagent's and general grocery at the corner and Bob Catchall, the landlord, when he collected the rent on Friday evening.

Wretched.

Pale and greasy and spotty and hairy. And dirty and smelly.

He felt better than he ever had before in his life. It was very bliss to be alive.

But dawn was long gone and the sun was all set to—well, set. Working like a dynamo, twenty hours a day, sometimes more, he was completing his thesis faster than he could ever have anticipated. In a matter of a month the draft was ready. Since it was not terribly long, the clean copy was typed within a week. He typed it himself, he was more than competent to do so, and why fork out a pound a page to some twit of a housewife banging away on some prehistoric machine on her kitchen table? (He'd visited some of the typists who advertised their services on the notice boards of Fairfield when Nuala had been getting her MA typed.) Then he had a shower, his first in weeks, ate a bowl of cornflakes and took the script, in three copies, to the binders: this necessitated a long journey to the north side of the city, a zone well off Erik's usual beat. But there were no corner copyshops in Dublin in those days: binding was a specialised esoteric

skill, practised up alleyways and down lanes in
far-off, impenetrable places. Erik, still high as a
gas balloon on his own immortal work,
welcomed the arduous journey as the intrepid
mountaineer greets the especially steep and
rugged peak.

The trip in the Number Twelve was the
journey of a lifetime. The Twelve was, as Nuala
had never tired of pointing out to him, an
exceptionally democratic bus, straddling
almost the entire Dublin social spectrum, from
the opulent villas of Palmerstown Park to the
Victorian slums of Charlemont Street, all the
way across to the new northside horrors of
Cabra corporation estates. No other bus
exposed itself to the rough and the smooth in
quite the same way. The Eleven and Thirteen,
for instance, also making the gallant trip from
south to north, avoided all but the most
salubrious urban and suburban areas, going to
elaborate and intricate lengths to do so. Erik
had half-listened to Nuala's theories—they
were not original, she had picked up all this
from a bus conductor she'd danced with once
at the Fairfield dance, years before she knew
Erik—and he had not regarded the matter as
one of the slightest importance or even interest.
But today he was in a mood to appreciate any
theory, however trivial. And how he savoured
this rolling view of life in the raw! Merrily he
rocked across the centre of the town, down
around Trinity (They'll be surprised! The

bastards!) across to Dorset Street, where the binder worked in a large warehouse on Basin Lane. With pride he selected a colour (black, his favourite) and left his script in the calloused hands of the foreman, a person of apparent erudition, who could no doubt have written a PhD himself, thought Erik, and said Erik, much to the other's gratification. With a light heart the real doctoral candidate walked home. Skipped hopped and walked, all along big grubby O'Connell Street, officious D'Olier Street, gloomy Georges Street, blowsy Camden Street, across the brave, down-at-heel bridge of Portobello and all the way up the slender confident thoroughfare of Rathmines to Frankfurt Avenue.

Then he collapsed on to his unmade bed, and into an abyss of depression.

His inside suddenly felt like the inside of the flat: empty, cold and infested by vermin.

I could clean it up.

I could go to Mrs Flynn's and buy a few traps. She must have some, mixed up with the bars of chocolate and the cream buns and the evening papers.

But the last thing he wanted to do was clean it up. Such a venture required a sturdy heart and a clear head. In his brain, lines of the poem, quotations from learned articles, authors and titles and page numbers, danced relentlessly. Andrew Higgins, 'Chaucer's theory of demonology in *The Canterbury Tales*, *The*

Chaucer Review, Vol. XXI, 1965, p. 214–237. 'Higgins's argument deserves careful consideration, but in light of the evidence presented in the previous chapter, can be criticised for the following reasons:...'

And more of the same.

He was in the undesirable, futile position of having in his mind all together and all at once every fact, every line, every thought, every half-thought, which had gone into the production of his thesis. If called upon to dispute it, he would have been able to recall effortlessly every commentary, every critical work he had consulted. But he was not being called upon to dispute it. He would not be. He would not be required to talk about this thesis ever again. It was finished. Only his head was prey to this mad circus of information, prancing, somersaulting, racing, driving him mad.

I could read Mother's letters.

There was a heap of them on the floor, four or five, which he had not opened.

Not now.

I could ring Binjy.

This idea had a certain appeal. A night in O'Neill's with Binjy could, if anything could, lay the ghosts. At the very worst he could get so polluted that he would be unable to think for at least a night and a day.

He rang Binjy's flat.

Binjy was not in. Binjy, suggested the high

falsetto voice which answered the phone, had gone away. He was, opined the voice, possibly in America. Home.

Finding another tenpenny piece in his pocket, Erik telephoned Vogue.

Vogue was in.

She did not say: 'Hello darling!'

She did not say: 'Hello stranger!'

She was, for Vogue, decidedly cool.

No, she could not meet him tonight for a drink. She had made other arrangements.

Yes, she would have coffee the day after tomorrow, at four o'clock in Bewley's on Grafton Street, downstairs.

Erik pulled the curtains against the strong evening sunshine, and went back to bed.

Nuala, to her discomfiture, received an invitation to Sean's wedding. It seemed that ever since she had lost Erik and begun to change her mind about the merits of marriage that she was to be forced to experience an *embarras de nuptiis*. The bells were ringing in her ears from morning till night, everywhere she went. Lest she forget, for a moment, what she was forfeiting.

There was the usual problem of what to wear. And, as usual, her overflowing wardrobe did not contain a single thing that was suitable. Mollie, an enthusiastic shopper, came to her aid and they spent an entire day in town searching the shops for the perfect outfit. The contents of

Clerys, Arnotts and Cassidys were reviewed and rejected. In the newer boutiques, like Mirror Mirror, and the little anonymous shops in the Dandelion Market, Mollie was ill-at-ease and a bad judge. Finally they found a suitable garment in Colette Modes, an unlikely source which Mollie disliked intensely.

'There's far too many people working in that place!' she said, as she always did whenever the name was mentioned. 'All rushing to help you. They get commission or something. If there's one thing I hate it's that, "Can I help you, Madam?" before you're inside the door.'

But they managed to elude the rapacious assistants long enough to select a flowing dress in black granny print and a wide black straw hat to match.

'Yes, it suits you, love!' Mollie said, appraisingly. 'The hat's gorgeous!'

It did not occur to either of them that black was an unusual choice of colour for a spring wedding. Mollie was not familiar with modern etiquette; when she had been a girl in the country most brides had worn navy-blue suits. Nuala had not been to many weddings and so was ignorant of the convention with ordained that pastels were essential. What she chiefly cared about was that the colour flattered her complexion and made her look thinner than she was. She would no doubt have plenty of opportunity to wear the dress when she got to Finland, on the scholarship which she had not

211

yet got around to applying for.

Do it first thing on Monday. Do not put it off any longer. The closing date is next Friday. Do not be a fool. And you've got to ask someone for a reference, which is horrible, absolutely horrible. I hate asking people for references more than anything else in the world.

Tommy gave her a lift from outside Easons to the wedding, which was to take place in Lucan. His wife, Marida, was in the passenger seat, and Elizabeth, Paul and Adèle from the office had already taken their places in the back. Pauline was making her own way, in her fiancé's car. Even without her, it was a tight squeeze in the yellow Renault 4. Tommy made jokes about the *Guinness Book of Records*, and Nuala squirmed, inwardly (it was impossible to do so outwardly in that car) and worried about her dress, which was being sat upon heavily on one side by Elizabeth and lightly on the other by Paul. (Adèle was on Elizabeth's lap). She wished she had tried to get to Lucan by some alternative means of transport. Surely there was a bus, even to such a distant place?

They arrived at the church with barely five minutes to spare. Many guests had assembled. They stood about the yard, in little groups, chatting. In their frocks of blue and lemon and pink, they looked like posies of flowers scattered on the grass under the spreading trees. The church itself was a gingerbread house, all tiny panes of coloured glass and cut

granite blocks. It was perched, in its delightful
grounds, on a terrace high above the Liffey,
which meandered, brilliantly blue out here,
through meadows and slopes, on to the stony,
pretty village of Lucan. The sun shone in the
full thin glow of a spring afternoon: the whole
scene was flooded in clear white light, like a
north-facing studio.

Oh, how lovely it is! The dress is not too
bad. That long wrinkle will come out. It's
beautiful, just beautiful! Lucky old Sean! If I
were marrying, I'd choose just this place, a
place just like this, with just such nicely attired
guests.

Upon closer scrutiny, the latter did not seem
so eminently desirable. Sugary dresses covered
bodies which were too fat or—less often—too
thin. Varicose veins bulged over pink satin
shoes, double chins sank into chiffon roses.
They had looked better in the soft focus of
distance. A less sunny day would have been
kinder, too, to spots and acne and facial hair.
The ideal wedding day would require a gentle
shading of cloud. Better, too, for the nostalgia,
the soft sepia tinting of the Victorian scene, the
Victorian institution. The happy couple.

Nuala, not knowing any of the other guests,
stayed with her colleagues, who commented on
the weather and the view and the
disadvantages of not being able to drive and
not being able to afford a car. Peter told a story
about a woman who had had a nasty

experience at a supermarket. While she was in shopping, something went wrong and she couldn't get her car started. A kind young man came up and offered to help. He examined the car, and found the cause of the problem. He offered a replacement part at a cost of thirty pounds. The woman was very glad to pay such a modest sum. She drove off happily.

The next day, exactly the same thing happened to her next door neighbour. It was all a con.

'That really happened. As true as God. It happened to a friend of Joe's. You know Joe, in Statistics? Him.'

A hand clamped Nuala's left shoulder.

'God! Professor Smyth! Hello.'

'Hi, Nuala, lovely to see you.'

John Smyth had an American accent, picked up during his years of study at Harvard.

'What are you doing here?'

Why should I be polite to the bastard anyway?

'Oh, I guess I've come to snatch away the bride—what do you think?' He laughed heartily. The laughter resounded in his capacious stomach and went booming around the churchyard. 'No, seriously, I am related to the bride. A third cousin, to be precise. Marriage to third cousins is permissible but not, I think, desirable.'

'No. Particularly if you happen to be married already.'

'Yes indeed.'

Boom boom boom.

He was a big man, with a long face, Rocky mountain nose, and a wide mouth. His hair was blond and curly. Could that be natural, at his age?

'And what, may I ask, are you doing here yourself?'

'I work with Sean. The groom.'

'Oh yes. In the Civil Service, isn't it? Which department now?'

'The European Environment.'

'Ah yes. Not a power position exactly, is it?'

Boom boom boom.

Rude as well.

'So, where is Mary? Didn't she want to come?'

'Well, I am the third cousin, not Mary, you know.'

'She's supposed to be your fiancée, isn't she?'

'Well, well.' He kicked a pine cone, which had lingered on the grass since autumn. His shoes were of old, scuffed suede.

'Well well!' said John Smyth again, flushing faintly. 'I did not expect to be attacked in this way at my third cousin's wedding. By the way, where is she? It's getting late, isn't it?'

It was a quarter past three by now. The entire wedding party was assembled on the lawn. It was getting quite crowded. Would they all fit in the church, Nuala wondered, glancing around. Sean she could see outside the porch, chatting to an elderly man, somebody's father, probably. Other people were looking over their shoulders, too, and even more were gazing down the roadway. The atmosphere, Nuala sensed suddenly, was becoming nervous. The pastel backs were too straight, strained. Some of the smiles were marred by frowns of anxiety. She even heard someone saying: 'Where is she? Really, we'll be late for the reception if this goes on.'

The elderly man talking to Sean was his own father. They had been joined, Nuala now saw, by the priest, in white and gold vestments. He kept looking at his watch.

'It's like that scene in *Women in Love,* isn't it? And I do believe Jenny has horses and a coach. What a pity you didn't wear green stockings and an artistic duckegg coat!'

'And that my sister didn't come!'

John Smyth ignored the remark.

'Another wedding at four, I believe!' he laughed. He had talked to a few of his cousins. 'If Jenny doesn't make it sharpish, she'll be in trouble.'

'She is already, isn't she?' Nuala spoke absently.

'In that sense? I shouldn't be surprised in the least.'

'Oh no…I meant…'

'But she is, no doubt. Why else…? But what can be happening?'

Twenty-five past three. Someone had gone to the vestry to telephone. The assembly, no longer pretending not to be perturbed, waited with bated breath for the result of the call.

Half past three.

The priest, traditional leader of the people, addressed the congregation from the porch.

'I am afraid that...'

Jenny had decided not to go through with it.

'Jesus, she must be cracked, that Jenny one!' Tommy, driving them all back to town, was indignant on Sean's behalf. Nobody had been brave enough to go near Sean. Indeed they had not seen him since a few minute's before the great announcement. He'd been spirited away, mercifully, before the final débâcle. All the pastel ladies climbing into their cars, disgruntled and cheated, their minds and tongues clicking. Paul and Adèle and the various pals and colleagues looking puzzled, or laughing anxiously, as they swung out of the gates. John Smyth chuckling lightly to himself as he walked down the hill towards the village bus-stop: he could not drive, he had informed Nuala, as he made a hasty goodbye.

'Well, darling, its probably better in the long run. I mean, better that she changes her mind now than next week when its too late.'

'For God's sake, woman, she's with child!'

With child. For God's sake. Where does he get them from?

'Oh!'

Marida's 'Oh' expressed shock, horror and disgust.

'Exactly: oh! What the hell is she going to do about that, I ask you?'

'There's always adoption,' said Marida, soothingly, as Tommy overtook a huge articulated truck just after the traffic lights at Kilmainham and narrowly avoided a collision with a bus.

'And abortion,' added Nuala, without thinking.

Tommy slammed on the brakes, as a four-year-old boy rushed across the road, waving a green fishing net in the air.

'Fucking little fool; old enough to watch where he's going, isn't he?'

'He's going to catch pinkeens, in the canal. Gosh, I remember doing that when I was a child. It was such fun. Did you ever do it, Tommy?'

Tommy made no audible reply.

'Children nowadays miss so much of the fun we used to have.'

'The simple things,' ventured Adèle, from under Elizabeth.

There was silence. Nobody could think of anything more to say until Tommy let Nuala out at the Ever Ready factory.

'See you on Monday,' she said. 'Thanks for the ride.'

He smiled coldly and nodded. She slunk away.

CHAPTER FIFTEEN

The strangest thing about the affair was that Sean turned up for work on Monday as if nothing untoward had occurred. Nuala had imagined that he might apply for a visa to emigrate to America or take the next plane to Hong Kong. Or, at the very least, she had expected him to succumb to a mild but lengthy dose of influenza. But no. There he was, early for once, head bent over his desk, carefully examining the contents of his in-tray.

Nobody mentioned the wedding, of course, until finally, before the first shift went up for teabreak in the canteen, he brought up the subject himself.

'I'm OK,' he said with a smile. He had humorous-looking eyes. Indeed, he always seemed to be manfully suppressing an urge to burst into a huge belly-laugh. Saturday's events had not altered this characteristic, which probably indicated that it was more of a physical than a temperamental trait. Don't judge a book by its cover. 'As a matter of fact, I'm relieved. It's all turned out for the best.'

Nobody said anything. Even Tommy was speechless. He gazed past Sean to the poster at the back of the room that depicted the river Corrib and a man reeling in a fat salmon, and proclaimed, mysteriously: 'A Cleaner Ireland for All!' One wondered if the salmon were some kind of undesirable pest, a carrier of unspeakable diseases or some imaginatively-shaped shaped piece of garbage. Just one more rotten fish.

'I wish it had happened earlier, so that so many people didn't have to be disappointed. But I've spoken to Jenny. She's OK, too, and sorry about the mess. And we're returning all the presents as soon as we have the energy to get around to it.' He had addressed them in a mild, simpering tone thus far. Now his voice darkened. 'So you don't have to worry about wasting your fucking money on a fucking non-starter like me, do you?'

And he got up from his desk and raced out of the room.

'Oh God!' said Tommy, his face coming to life all of a sudden, like a television that has just been switched on. He rushed out too.

Steps could be heard pounding rapidly down the wooden stairs. For some reason neither of them had thought to use the lift. Perhaps it was out of order. It frequently was. Everyone dashed over to the window and looked on to the street, except for Paul who ran out the door, saying: 'I want a grandstand seat!' The others stood holding back the plastic blind for about five minutes but nothing happened.

Neither Sean nor Tommy emerged.

'They probably went to the car-park,' murmured Pauline, nonplussed but with a barely perceptible note of disappointment in her voice. The car-park was under the building in a large grey basement, and the exit therefrom was invisible from the vantage point of the office.

Accepting this pessimistic view of the matter, they all went up for tea, leaving the phones unattended, which was against the rules. There were a lot of awkward rules in the Department, some silly and antediluvian, others sensible and antediluvian. This was one of the factors which had depressed Nuala greatly initially, until she realised that hardly anybody paid any attention to them in practice.

Tommy returned to the office an hour later, just as the tea-break finished and the last clerical officer was adjusting her skirts on her typing chair. Sean did not return that day and was on sick leave for the rest of the week. His coat and belongings (one large yellow canvas bag) disappeared mysteriously from the office during lunch hour. The consensus was that Tommy had taken them to Sean's flat. When the jilted bridegroom again made a appearance at work, people went out of their way to be tactful with him. He was never asked to contribute to collections for wedding presents or even retirement or resignation presents, lest this evoke insalutory memories. Topics relating to engagements, weddings, girlfriends, wives, women and children were never broached in his presence. This meant, in effect, that all young people were eternally silent when in his company. In consequence, he began to seek the companionship of his older colleagues, with whom he could converse about football results, by-elections and the death of Michael Collins. Within a short time, he was promoted to a position in the Department of Finance, a serious organ of government, unlike the Department of the European Environment, which, everyone knew, could be abolished at any Taoiseach's whim and its staff reallocated to the Revenue Commissioners. Thereafter his career progressed meteorically. He never returned the wedding presents. It was universally and resentfully assumed that his bedsit was exceptionally well-equipped, decked out with Waterford glass and canteens of Newbridge cutlery and luxurious pink bath-sheets, their corners embroidered in swirling satin thread with the tear-jerking designations, 'His' and 'Hers'. Or perhaps Jenny had held on to the loot. These questions, on many minds, were never asked, much less answered.

Not that Nuala worried unduly about where her fiver's worth had ended up. Because very soon after the wedding, just a week after sending in her application, she received a notification from Helsinki informing her that her application had been successful. She was cordially invited to take a place on their post-graduate course beginning on 4 September.

She was overjoyed at the news.

Quite bowled over.

So absolutely thrilled that she ran all around the block. Up Leinster Road, down Effra Road. Back up Leinster Road to the flat. And all around again. Twice.

She had to tell somebody.

She simply could not contain this stupendous piece of good fortune within the walls of her own frail mind. Out it must go, and quickly.

But in whom could she confide?

Not the girls in the office.

Not Jean, who would be envious and disapproving.

Not her mother (or father, needless to add).

And no. Not him.

The only living human being who might possibly respond with some sympathy to this information was Mary.

She didn't have Mary's phone number. Probably Mary did not have a phone. So she called John Smyth in his office in Fairfield and asked him if he could tell her how to get in touch with her sister.

And in this way he was the first to hear the breathtaking news.

'Congratulations!' he said, in his deep ironic tones, taking half the good out of it immediately.

He explained that they did not have a phone, as she had guessed, but he invited her around to their house that very evening, and she accepted the invitations with alacrity. Two birds with one stone. She'd been dying to see their place for months.

10 Avondale Terrace, off the South Circular Road, looked much as she had expected it to look: shabby and Victorian, exactly like her parents' house as far as structure was concerned. But it had a consoling sense of promise where the Byrne home hinted strongly at decay. An aura of impending prosperity and trendiness floated over number ten, as it did over the street as a whole. The concrete manifestions of this atmosphere were a small restaurant with red gingham curtains on the windows and a tiny French menu pinned to the door, and window boxes on a few of the houses. Number Ten was one of the latter, and displayed a respectable host of daffoldils, fluttering in the fumes from the traffic which plied the road rather mercilessly. Avondale Terrace was not quite an up-market area. There were no yuppies living on it as yet (mainly because as a breed they did not yet exist). It lacked patios, double-glazing, shrubs in tubs. Wealth. But you could tell at a glance that it was on the way up. Just as you would suspect that Exeter Place was going in the opposite direction. (Leinster Road, on the other hand, never went anywhere at all, socially, although

geographically it continued to play an important role, linking the ever more salubrious suburbs of Harold's Cross and Rathmines).

Mary's house, or John's house, had, as well as the daffodils, oriental matchstick blinds and a thick oak door. Its exterior was decidedly inviting. But that belied what lay within, which was innumerable varieties of squalor. The rooms were uncarpeted and had floors which might have been better concealed from view. The walls, on the contrary, were covered with ghastly paper patterned with monstrous cabbage roses and other, worse monstrosities. The furniture, what there was of it, was chipboard stuff with fake wood surfaces. But mainly there was no furniture.

'Yes,' said John with a smile, catching her expression. 'It is a trifle bare, isn't it? My wife held on to all the furniture, damn her!'

'Oh!' said Nuala. 'I see.'

If he's been divorced for years and years, how come he's got no new furniture? Every new comment on this man's marital status is turning out to be a fresh blow. Damn him.

'Well, she probably needed it more than you did, at the time!' intercepted Mary, who had just entered the hallway.

Taking the first wife's part? Isn't that a bit odd?

'With all the kids and everything!' Nuala let this slip out almost, although not, of course, quite, involuntarily.

Mary laughed carelessly and John managed a tight smile.

'So you've heard the gossip, have you?' Mary asked. 'Well, we've no secrets from anyone. It's not as if John never looks after the children, or anything. We'll take them…As a matter of fact, we do take them some of the time already. Half the time, to be exact.'

John slipped out of the room on some domestic errand. To fetch a baby or two?

'Really?'

If she'd said she had five children herself, Nuala would have now responded with a dispassionate 'really?'

'Well, we have them Friday to Sunday and she has them the rest of the time.'

Friday to Sunday. Technically a day less than half the week. In real terms about one quarter thereof? Or less?

'That sounds like a reasonable arrangement,' lied Nuala, her sympathy switching to the first wife. Monday to Thursday. Parent-teacher meetings. Swimming lessons. If…

'What ages are they?'

'The eldest is eight and the youngest is one and a half.'

'But…' John was coming out of the front room, carrying a wooden tray of wineglasses and a bottle. 'I thought he'd been divorced for years and years.'

'Two years. The youngest was a kind of

accident, wasn't she, John? He's not even sure if she's his,' she added confidentially.

'Red or white?' asked John solemnly.

'Red,' said Nuala. There was only red. He poured it out, half-filling each glass, a habit Nuala regarded with suspicion. Then he raised his drink high in the air.

'Congratulations, Nuala!' He continued to be solemn. Well he might.

Mary raised her glass and so did Nuala.

'And here's to the new baby!'

They all laughed very giddily, drained their glasses and then went into the kitchen for dinner.

The kitchen was not too disgusting. Indeed, it was the best room in the house, probably because its shoddy skeleton was disguised by a variety of interesting-looking foods and utensils, garnered from one knew not where: copper fish-kettles, painted paté pots, strings of onions and garlic, dressed up the broken tiles and battered shelves and gave the place what the rest of the house sadly lacked: atmosphere. The effect—of a cheap Mediterannean bistro— was enhanced by the red gingham tablecloth and the numerous bottles of wine on a rack by the door.

They ate something Provençal, with a lot of tomato and beans and a small amount of meat, and drank some bottles of wine. Nuala, ever the considerate guest, had brought a bottle of Beaujolais (she was at a Beaujolais age) and

John, it turned out, made wine. As a hobby. (Or because he was an alcoholic?) They got quite tipsy and Nuala began to feel very happy. What an excellent idea it had been, telling Mary about her good fortune! Nobody else of her acquaintance would have reacted so positively: everyone would have had some minor personal reservation, some greater existential worry, to tarnish their response. They would all have been piqued, to a greater or lesser extent. But Mary, who might have been forgiven for showing a spot of resentment, had none at all. It was not that she concealed her true feelings. She never did conceal any feelings; she could not do so. But she was simply genuinely delighted that Nuala was throwing up her boring job, that she was about to embark on a new course of study, that she was going to the Finland. John had been to a conference once, in Helsinki; he'd had a wonderful time. Yes, said John, yes he had. But he had little to tell of the experience. His conversation, indeed, was extremely banal, much more mundane than Nuala would have expected of a professor. If such people had nothing startling and vital and deep to say, who did? She was beginning to doubt very seriously that such a thing as good conversation existed. Or was it that the fault lay on her side? Maybe I'm so boring and dull and stupid and uninteresting and ordinary that people who would otherwise sparkle dry up in my presence? She thought. And drank another glass of wine. Oh, bitter bitter draught, home-made wine!

What John did talk about was the food, notably garlic and parsley.

'Parsley is supposed to contain a cure for colds,' he said. 'And that's good, because I've got one.'

'I grow it myself, you know,' said Mary, pointing at a tiny bed set in the middle of the yard. In the middle of the bed was a tiny green fountain. Parsley.

The talk turned to garlic and other cures for the common cold.

'When Sammie was two she had whooping cough, and we brought her out to sniff tar. We brought her to a place where roadworkers were spreading tar and let her sniff it for all she was worth.'

'Did it work?' asked Mary.

'No,' said John. 'But she enjoyed the experience. Tar is the sort of thing children love.'

Sammie was obviously one of his many children. He must have been pretty drunk to mention her so casually by name. Nuala found it unnerving, the realisation that he had been through whooping cough, that he knew intimate facts about children, such as that they liked tar. It seemed unfair that he should be embarking on the whole experience of marriage and fatherhood for the second time, while Mary was getting her first, and probably only, go. The

cat with nine lives. Theoretically he could drop
Mary and go and start off again in a few years'
time if the opportunity arose. Though twice on
that merry-go-round would probably be
sufficient for anyone, expecially in a fairground
like this, thought Nuala, eyeing the decor
critically. When the light went on the kitchen
looked as bad as the rest of the house. There
was a long crack snaking up one of the walls
and the lino simply looked dirty. And that big
porcelain sink might seem interesting and
Victorian in an antique dealer's but in this
kitchen it looked like what it was: an
incubation centre for germs, a sort of germ zoo.
It's a wonder they survive at all in the dump,
she thought, taking her leave and running to
catch the last bus home.

CHAPTER SIXTEEN

Nuala had mentioned to John and Mary that she was planning to learn some Finnish before she went to Helsinki, and had already bought a copy of *Teach Yourself Finnish*. John, ever unpredictable, had mentioned the gap in Nuala's education to Robin Allgood, and a few weeks after the celebratory dinner Robin telephoned her at her office and offered to give her Finnish lessons: as it happened, he had learned this language as a hobby some years previously. 'Just for fun, you know,' he said, with his little chuckle. 'I always wanted to know at least one language that is not Indo-European. And the grammar is very attractive. It's so delightfully complex.' Nuala was taken by surprise but she was glad to take Robin up on his offer; without analysing why, she found it flattering and encouraging. They arranged to meet in his room once a week, starting on the second of May. Nuala had already learnt something by the time the day of the lesson dawned. Robin, who had never considered her outstandingly bright, in spite of what she had imagined, was impressed. He suggested that she begin at the deep end by trying to read a novel with the aid of a dictionary.

'The one novel every Finn will expect you to know is this one.' He flashed a worn volume in front of her. '*Seven Brothers*. But it is quite hard going. You might prefer to try this.' And he showed her a new red paperback. 'I've only skimmed through it myself, I have to admit, and really it is not quite my cup of tea. But it is the latest craze, apparently, in Finland. The theme might interest a young person like you. '

He stared at her.

'Well, what is it called?' she asked.

'Translated roughly, *Men Cannot Be Raped*.'

'Gosh!' was all Nuala could come up with.

'Yes, it is what is called a feminist novel, I believe. Are you a feminist?'

'Well, you know, I don't kn…I don't think one should be a slave to feminism, or to anything else,' she said, priggishly, not knowing what the right answer to this one was.

Robin laughed. 'It will probably do you good to read this book then. Anyway the Finnish is easier than in *Seven Brothers* and I haven't got anything else except for the *Kalevala*, which I could not recommend at this stage.'

'All right,' said Nuala. 'Let's do this one.'

Nuala, doubting that his method could be successful, was nevertheless vain enough to begin to plod through the book with the aid of a large paperback dictionary. It was hard going. She had to look up almost every word, and it took her at least an hour to read half a page. Normally not a patient person, she applied herself to this task with unprecedented enthusiasm. Every evening as soon as she escaped from the office she rushed home, made a pot of coffee and sat by her window perusing the uncompromising text. She couldn't appreciate the style or even the narrative for a long time: maybe it was a good story; maybe it offered some novel insight into a problem which Nuala had barely heard of—rape: she knew about it in relation to the Sabine women but obviously it was not something which ever occurred in Ireland. Probably Finland was different.

She did not dwell on this thought. She was getting so immersed in the task in hand that nothing except that concerned her for long. Her thirst for Finnish was insatiable. She had spent the best part of a year in intellectual stagnation, and now she realised how she had missed flexing her brain cells. She had always been aware that she enjoyed studying but in a way she had been ashamed of this and had considered it an unnatural, unfeminine, almost an inhuman, pleasure. Learned people were as a rule dowdy or old or eccentric. Out of touch with reality. She did not want to be like them. She was not like them. But she could see how they became like that, all right. Learning new things was exciting. The hours spent by the window, checking words in the dictionary, were periods of intense happiness for her. Her chair was comfortable; her coffee was hot; gradually she was beginning to enjoy the shimmer of the words and, eventually, the story. Outside, soft summery air flowed through tender trees and the street wore its happiest, freshest aspect; inside the oxygen of grammar invigorated her mind. Her whole personality, her body, flourished under its influence. She felt herself reborn.

The highpoint of the week was the meetings with Robin. She sat at one side of his large desk and he at the other. She translated chunks of the novel and he corrected her and explained points of grammar. At the end of an hour, he congratulated her on her progress and said goodbye.

This, at least, had been the pattern of the first three meetings. After the fourth, he had changed the formula by inviting her for a drink in the common room and she had accepted eagerly. Robin was such a good teacher; he was such a decent bloke. She was getting quite fond of him. It would be nice to get to know him, although really she doubted if that were possible.

During the first and subsequent drinks— because the practice became a habit—she concluded, with more disappointment than she would have anticipated, that it was not. Shyness was not the problem: Robin was a fluent talker, and rattled on easily and sometimes wittily about Finland and feminism and his teaching and his research. But he remained reserved about himself, and so did she. Once their working relationship ceased, they had nothing of any importance to say to one another. There was a barrier which indicated that they were not, in fact, friends, although she did not understand what precisely was causing the block. He did not, it was true, appear to listen very carefully to anything she had to say which was not in Finnish. Frequently she caught him asking questions relating to her experiences and plans which she had answered several times before. But she had learned that most of the men she knew were inclined to act as if they were partially deaf and extremely absentminded. This had never hindered the development of romance in the past. Such men, it seemed, were able to make friends or to fall in love with one nevertheless. Not listening to half the things she said did not deter them in the least.

But with Robin it did. They were not getting close, although Nuala was feeling the tiny pleasant pinpricks of awakening interest in him. She had always liked him and considered him attractive in a slightly odd, outmoded way. Now she began to appreciate the finer details of his appearance and character. The slight hesitancy, hardly a stammer, in his speech, seemed touchingly sweet. The rough oily smell of his tweed jacket became raw and sexy, instead of faintly offensive. Even his glasses, very old-fashioned ugly ones such as boys on the National Health wore in the 1950s, struck her as being strongly individualistic rather than an eyesore. Robin, after all, was too intellectual and unworldy to care about such things as fashionable spectacles. He was above all base materialism. And so, now, was Nuala. Her true vocation, learning, had been rediscovered. Along with what she liked to regard as her first true disinterested affection for a truly noble fellow creature. Robin. No longer odd. Just good.

Robin Hood, Robin Hood, riding through the glen

Robin Hood, Robin Hood, with his band of men...

She was singing this song, remembered from childhood television-watching in Exeter Place, one Saturday evening as she took a short break from her Finnish in order to tidy up the flat. Just as she was scrubbing the kitchen sink with a broken pad of steel wool, which exuded finger-hostile pink soap and spiky scraps of vicious grey wire, the doorbell rang. Not bothering to dry her hands, she went downstairs to answer it.

And there he stood.

Erik.

'Come in,' said Nuala, ATP. 'Hello, hello, please come in.'

He stepped into the hall and she wiped her hands on the backside of her jeans, standing against the wall, which was painted a startling Mary, Queen of Heaven blue.

'How are you?' he said.

His voice was dry and tense, as it had been in the days when she had first met him. And his face looked as it had then, too: white, taut, spotty. And beautiful.

'Oh, I'm fine. Would you like to come in for a cup of coffee?' she said.

'Yes. That would be nice,' he said.

'Well…' she said.

And led the way.

Thus she fell into the maw of temptation, headlong, up to her ears, precipitated there by her own deficiencies. Her insecurity, her uncertainty, her inhibitions, her understandings and several more 'in's and 'un's. Dogged by misgivings, she pattered up the bare stairs with Erik trudging purposefully along in her wake.

He sat in the best armchair, not taking off his coat. What do you want a coat for on a day like this? It's June, Erik, it's twenty-one degrees. You look like an abominable snowman; you look as if you haven't been out of your den since last February.

You look lovely.

Nuala busied herself boiling water. The devil does not find work for occupied hands. Keep them busy, spoon in the coffee, try to open that carton of milk without using a scissors. Bite the cardboard, bite it. Drat, it won't work. Ask...no, not yet, that's it. The breadknife. Saw off the damp little corner.

'Bikkies?'

Bikkies, indeed. She never used words like that. When she was nervous, she often found herself slipping into somebody else's speech patterns.

Erik busied himself snooping among her books and papers.

He quickly found what he was looking for.

'You're reading Finnish?'

The inquisition began. How could he fail to notice the book, the dictionary, the accumulating notebooks full of new words, the tape recorder? The whole bedsit was full of this stuff.

But of course it wasn't as simple as that. Not by a long shot. He'd known she was learning Finnish before he'd set foot in the flat. She knew it must be so. How did he know it? She did not know. People got to find out such things. Such things...as someone learning Finnish. From someone like Robin Allgood, who was an English teacher, godammit, so why the hell is he teaching her Finnish, he doesn't even know Finnish properly, it takes the biscuit, it really does.

'Yes.'

Nuala handed him a cup.

Erik took the cup and placed it, carefully, on the floor. All his movements were slow and careful. That was the type of character he was.

'I've heard about the scholarship. Congratulations.'

His eyes. Oh those eyes, those old blue eyes. Blue as ice, blue as skies, blue as duckeggs, blue for a boy, blue, blue, your eyes are blue. Old Blue Eyes is back blue. Blues blue. Bluebag blue.

They were often hard, they were often cold, they were often piercing, they were often—yes, let's face it—cruel.

Now they were just blue.

Melting. Vulnerable. Hurt, hurt. Hurt.

'Thank you.'

Oh I am sorry, I'm sorry, I'm sorry. I didn't mean to hurt you, I didn't mean to get a scholarship and annoy you, you poor soft old blue-eyed creature you.

'Yeah, it's great. And you're learning Finnish already. Great! What are you doing, going to classes?'

He knows.

'Well no. Someone's helping me…giving me lessons.'

'Who?'

Hyacinths. Piercing. Hitler had eyes like that. Smaller and meaner but with that gimlet look. I bet.

'Robin Allgood.'

'That's very kind of him, isn't it?'

'Yes.'

He drank some coffee. 'So you're really

going then?'

'Well, yes, I am.'

Of course I'm going. Of course I am.

'Good.'

He drank more coffee.

'You're giving up your job?'

'Yes.'

'Mmm. I hope you know what you're doing.'

Well, honestly!

Honestly?

He cares, he cares. He doesn't want me to go.

Oh, my God. Oh, mother of God! He cares about me!

He looks awful.

Haggard and worn and tense and tired. His clothes are filthy. His hair looks mouldy. He hasn't shaved in days.

Obviously…

He lit a cigarette.

'You smoke now?'

He loves me.

'It's fun. Want one?'

'No thanks.'

'So, how have you been?'

Cheery down at the farm voice.

'Busy. With the flat and everything.'

'I like the flat. It is a good idea, the flat.'

And I love him.

'I like living here.'

He placed his mug carefully on the floor and

put his arms carefully around her shoulders.

'I have missed you.'

He's got eyes of blue and that's my weakness now.

'I've missed you too.'

The scholarship, Helksinki, the man who was raped, dissolved. Unreality, how various are your manifestations! Sublimation of desire, how subtle are your workings! Happy, have I been happy? Not for a moment, not for half a moment, not for the minutest particle of an hour. It was all self-deception, hastily woven garments to keep out the cold brutal reality of the case.

'Oh, I missed you so much!'

And so on and so forth. Into his arms. Into bed. Up to her neck into it all.

And then he went. Sunday passed. Monday passed. Tuesday passed. And Erik did not come back.

Nuala continued to work at her translation. But although the novel was getting more and more fascinating, and her mastery of the language better and better, her heart was no longer in the work. She tried but her concentration slipped. Her ear was cocked all the time. He might ring. He might call round. It had been understood— by her—that he would, although he had made no specific date. Hell, he was busy. He loved her he'd be around.

Her heart thumped against her ribs. In fear

(Sunday and Monday: what did I do wrong? Why isn't he here?). In anger (Tuesday: the dirty double-crosser).

Wednesday was Robinday.

The heroine of the novel—a librarian— celebrated her fortieth birthday alone in a singles bar. Her husband had left her four years earlier. Her lover had gone back to his wife. She was forty and alone in a bar, drinking wine.

Nuala could not imagine being forty. Caring about men when you were forty. Being involved in love and betrayal and all that stuff. Shouldn't it all be over, well over, at that stage? In Ireland it would be, she was sure of it. In Ireland you'd be ancient, at forty.

Robin told Nuala that he was going away.

Away!

People like him do go away. To conferences. To libraries. To give lectures in far-off lands.

To visit his mother.

Funny how they all have mothers tucked away somewhere.

'My mother lives outside Birmingham. Hadn't I mentioned her before? I spend a few weeks with her whenever I can. She's on her own, you know. I'm all she has, so to speak.'

'When are you going?'

'Next week.'

And he invited her to dinner. On the following Saturday, in a restaurant in Dalkey.

Erik was, meanwhile, lying on the broad of

his back in his room on Frankfurt Avenue, suffering from something which he guessed to be food poisoning. He had eaten fish and chips on his way home from Nuala's on Saturday night, and blamed them. His stomach was racked by terrible cramps, his head span crazily whenever he left his bed to go to the loo. He thought he would probably die.

Just as well, too. There was nothing to live for. His thesis was finished, and he would in due course be told that it had passed and that he would be conferred with the degree of PhD. So what? There were no jobs available and he had nowhere to go. Home, which he had longed for before Christmas, now seemed more forbidding than almost anywhere else in the world. He had broken off all communications with his mother: Several months' letters lay in a heap under his bed, unopened. Recently they came less and less frequently; she was giving up on him. Good! The sooner they severed the connection the better. He'd had enough.

Vogue was busily doing examinations at school, something called the 'Leaving' which she took very seriously indeed. She had refused to see him for a month prior to the thing, and now she had been doing it for at least a month, and had met him only twice. He was tiring of her in any case. She was pretty but silly and schoolgirlish. Her interests—apart from the Leaving—were featherheaded. All she cared about was money and the things money can buy. And then she never spent any of her own when she was with him. Mean is what she was. He wasn't that interested.

And now Nuala was going to Finland and, in the meantime, having some sort of stupid affair with that wimp, Robin Allgood. A man old enough to be her father, almost. A crusty old bachelor, as odd as two left shoes. Must be forty at least. What he needed was a nurse-maid, not a girlfriend.

Not a wife.

Who mentioned wives? Nuala was going to Finland on some silly course for comparative literature. Who needs a course on that? Some sort of non-subject invented by a universities anxious to attract stupid students with more money than brains.

That Robin Allgood was a creep. As soon as he saw his chance, he moved in. Who would have guessed Nuala could be in such demand? Well, she was pretty, of course, and quite intelligent, and nice. Nuala was so nice. She'd reacted so well to his mother and that horrible Elsa. How would Vogue have taken it? He shuddered to think. Or anyone else. But Nuala took it in her stride. She hadn't batted an eyelid, she'd gone out of her way to be nice. That was the advantage of people with her sort of background. They never really knew what was what and they were always a bit servile, a bit anxious to please. But that wouldn't be such a bad thing, in a wife...Wife, who's talking about wives? Nuala's going to Finland. She wants a career, for heaven's sakes. She's liberated, she's a bloody women's libber, she's just the wrong sort of person to marry. Marriage? Who's talking about marriage?

He wished he could telephone her. But the coinbox in the hall was out of order, as usual, and he simply didn't have the strength to get up and go out to find a phone. God, if I don't get in touch with her soon she'll think...she'll go to him...she'll marry him tomorrow...oh my God. I wish, I wish...

On Thursday, he felt slightly better, and got up. His legs wobbled at first and his face in the mirror looked quite green but after a half an hour or so he began to feel more human. A bath he considered, but could not face the ordeal. In his condition, in that bathroom, it might be very dangerous. So he contented himself with washing down with a sponge, dampening and brushing his hair, and dressing in the cleanest jeans and shirt he possessed. At the last minute he found a bottle of shaving lotion which Elsa, goddamher, had given him at Christmas. Brut. Brute yourself Elsa.

So when Nuala came home from work, at half past five, there he was.

He explained and she accepted the explanation but she had a faraway look in her eye which he interpreted as a danger sign. He suggested they go for a walk.

Nuala liked walking.

They walked along Leinster Road as far as Harold's Cross, and then they passed through the village to the green in the middle of the road. And there they sat on a park bench, and observed some children at play on the swings.

It was a beautiful evening, like all the evenings of that summer. The park reminded Nuala of Elizabeth Bowen, whom she was reading in the breaks from the rapist. She mentioned this to Erik.

What an interesting woman she is! She reads things, she remembers things, not just lists of facts for examinations.

'Don't go to Finland, Nuala,' he said, staring at her earnestly.

'What?

I'm going. He might as well ask me to cancel the new year, or to forget the rest of my life. I'm going to Finland. It is a fact, not an opinion that can be changed.

'Don't go. Its a waste of time, and it's silly to give up your job and everything. And, I would like you to stay.'

Well. It's nice to hear that.

'I've missed you so much. I made a terrible mistake, I really did. Please forgive me for that, but try to understand why I did it.'

'Why?'

'Because I felt we were getting claustrophobic. I felt we needed to broaden out horizons and so on. I explained to you at the time. And I never meant it to be permanent. I did say that.'

'Yes, you did. But I didn't believe you.'

'You should have. You should have had more faith in me.

'I'm sure you're right.'

'Yes, I am. But it's all right now. I know what I feel I know where I stand. I want you so much. I'll miss you so much if you go.'

Haven't I heard this before somewhere? From someone? From Erik?

'Do you think you could change your mind?'

'I'm not sure.'

I'm not sure. I could. Old Blue Eyes is back. He looks so wonderful, in that blue shirt. I did love him so much. I mean he is right for me, I think. But could I trust him? Wouldn't he do the same thing again?

'I'd have to think about it.'

His grip on her shoulder tightened and he smiled peaceably to himself. Unconsciously he heard his mother murmuring, 'We'll see,' to some outrageous childhood request of his. Her 'We'll sees' had always meant one thing when it came to the crunch. He closed his blue eyes on the shimmering blue sky, the midges circling like stars in the golden dust, and the deep June green trees. He closed his eyes on Nuala.

CHAPTER SEVENTEEN

Thursday was the day of reunion. A good day—confusing, certainly, but gratifying as well. Friday was the day after, sabre-toothed. Nuala at work did not work—as usual—but did it in a more nervous manner than had been her custom over the past few months. Nuala at home tackled her Finnish. Lene invited a man she'd met in the bar in for a cup of coffee. The man raped her. Nuala wondered. The man assumed he could go to bed with her because she had asked him in. A forty-year-old mother of two in Finland, with a marriage and three lovers behind her. Was that rape? Nuala had never been pushed into bed by somebody. But she'd been kissed violently against her will; she'd been assaulted in a car when she took a lift to a country town. She'd had complete strangers feel her legs in a cinema and once, even, crossing O'Connell Street at lunchtime. She'd never even thought of mentioning any of this to anyone. It had upset her at the time and had felt shameful. But she'd also regarded it as trivial, presumably commonplace. One of the unpleasant things that happened to you, like getting slaps in school. If you went to school, if you took a lift from a stranger, if you danced with a man all night, certain things would be expected. That you hadn't anticipated them in time was your own fault. Wasn't it? As a woman you should know where to go and what to do; you should know the consequences of everything. No use crying over spilt milk.

Hysterical. That's what it was.

The whole novel seemed hysterical and improbable, steeped in prejudice, silly. Silly feminist novel. Doesn't understand that men are just human too, that they are not monsters, out to assault, abuse, betray.

Erik is not a monster. It's not his fault that he has problems making up his mind. I have problems with that too. And Robin is more or less an angel.

She tossed it aside and the dictionary after it, and started to cry.

She hadn't cried in weeks. Not since she'd started learning Finnish. Almost four weeks of calm industriousness. And now she was back in the land of tears again. The real world?

Dust settled over the streetscape, which until today had been clean and dewy-fresh. The summer is going, she said to herself, twice, aloud. The summer is going. And she did not think, 'I am going too!', a thought which would have cheered her up yesterday or the day before, the thought which had kept her going for months. When she tried to think of anything, she found herself foundering into a mess of tangled wires. Who? Where? Why? So those wires were called. Erik and Robin and Finland and Career and Life and If and Then. She found herself stumbling in a dark forest instead of floating through light crystal air, flying westwards like an occidental swallow from the winter wiles of the old rotten cruel eastern world, as she had been a week before. She did not have a compass. She did not speak the language of the natives.

Erik called around late on Friday. She managed to get rid of him before morning, although it was not easy. He needed to talk through everything. He needed to be with her. He needed her sympathy, and he got it—of course he got it. But Saturday she needed to have to herself, to prepare for the evening ahead.

When she woke up, she found herself relieved and light-headed, as she always was on Saturdays, no matter how traumatic Friday night had been.The day stretched ahead, empty of work, empty of Erik, and empty, for the duration, of problems. Day of the week! She lay in bed, watching the bars of sunshine which lined the floor grow yellower and stickier, and wished all of life could be a series of such periods of rest, peace, blissful solitude. A life lacking all decisions and choices and jobs and men seemed eminently desirable. It occurred to her that, since it was possible for her to forget about them on Saturdays, it should be possible to forget about them always, given a little self-discipline and effort. Perhaps people who were truly serene had that ability. Perhaps that's what serenity was, what happiness was? But the infeasibility of it struck her soon enough, before she'd finished her toast and coffee, which she took, according to custom, sitting up in bed.

The coffee, perhaps, having provided her start of the day nervous shock, suggested that life could not be so peaceful unless one were prepared to forego considerably more than she was likely to want to let go of. Nuns in contemplative orders, probably, enjoyed the Saturday morning feeling all the time. That's what life in a contemplative order must be: one long Saturday. One long nothing. But could an ordinary person stand it? Could she? Because part of the thrill of the ordinary Saturday sensation was its very transitoriness and the contrast between it and the rushed and snarled times. If there were no such contrast, what then? And another part of the Saturday feeling was the anticipation of its urbane pleasures: the walk to town, the Dandelion Market, the coffee in Bewleys, *The Irish Times*, the dahlias in Stephen's Green: modest treats, perhaps, but not the kind one was likely to enjoy immured in the Enclosed Carmelites or the Poor Clares. The high walls of their convents (there was one in Ranelagh, under the railway bridge, not far from Mollie's and Dessie's house) held no attraction for her. The sight of those walls, huge and grim like the walls of a high security prison, had always repelled her. The convent was a fortress in the middle of a perfectly ordinary city village: outside its walls was the shoemaker's shop, and opposite a small greengrocer. Those impenetrable walls, were they designed to keep the nuns in or the villagers out? Did they fear the shoemaker, a mild bald man in a brown coat to which the bitter smell of leather clung? Or was it the greengrocer? He was truculent, red-haired, always ready to snap a customer's head off. Anyone could have justifiably tried to keep him away. From men of evil temper the good Lord deliver us. The nuns knew, perhaps, what they were doing. But the thought of them now sobered her and made her feel momentarily grateful for Erik and his foibles, Robin and his elusive promise, the future in its irksome uncertainty. Her life was full, after all, at the moment—if nothing else. She felt smug, thinking of it. Chockful of possibility. Rich, in a way, is what it was. Special, in a way, is what she was. A very special individual.

She was to meet Robin at his flat in Dun Laoghaire, and they were going to go together to the restaurant he had chosen in Dalkey.

She bathed and dressed with great care, choosing something which she felt made her look beautiful in an ultra-feminine way. Her idea of ultra-femininity had reverted to the romantic after her flirtation with the stylish in Copenhagen. Now her smart aggressive clothes bored her, and she favoured the modest and girlish and chintzy rather than the sexy. So she decked herself up in a white print dress, pure as the flowers of May, and brushed her hair out so that it glittered like a rich red cloak over her shoulders. On her feet she wore natural leather thonged sandals, and she carried a straw basket, containing a purse and a brush and— for safety's sake—a powder puff. Over her shoulders she hung a white wool coat which she believed made her look rich and cared-for. Thus attired, she set off, walking to Ballsbridge to catch the Number Eight bus, the same route she had travelled last November on her way to the party in Monkstown, the first of Erik's betrayals. Ah, life, so full of tiny malicious ironies!

It was bright now so she was able to enjoy the trip much more than she had done then. A bus-ride in summer is quite a different thing from one on a dark winter's night, and she found the experience redolent of trips to Sandymount with Mollie during summer holidays long ago—a positive association. Besides, she was used to being alone on buses, alone everywhere, now, and the experience caused her no misgivings whatever. She was not, however, conscious of the alteration in her general attitude to life. She had already forgotten how miserable and frightened she had been that night in November, before Erik had said one word to her, before she had known he was sick and tired of her. All she recalled was that it had been cold and that she hadn't been able to see anything, and that the journey had seemed long and ennervating. Whereas now she stared happily at passing houses and gardens, at canoes in the water at Seapoint and cormorants on the rocks outside Dun Laoghaire. Before she knew where she was, she was getting off the bus and walking along in the light sea breeze towards Miranda Terrace, where Robin lived.

It was on the seafront, just before People's Park, he had told her. So she walked along the promenade, which was all very gay and cheerful: Chinese lanterns hung from the trees lining the footpath, boats bobbed about in the harbour, people strolled along, smiling and seemingly carefree. But as she came nearer to Miranda Terrace, something strange began to happen to her stomach. It wound itself into a hard knot inside her. Her legs felt weak, and she knew her face, liberally covered with make-up, was much paler than ivory—the make up was called 'Pale Ivory.' She felt green. She had to sit down at one point just to recover her wits and her strength. She could hardly walk.

It's only dinner. It's only dinner, for Gods sake; it's nothing serious. Don't be such a wimp. Don't turn every mountain into a molehill. Go and have dinner with the man and forget it! He's off to England next week. You don't ever have to see him again.

The sea winked, sly as a sapphire, at her. The sun shone pale and penetratingly from the white-blue sky.

Fortified by her pep talk, she got up and walked doggedly on. 5 Miranda Terrace pounced upon her before she expected it: it was on the corner of the street. The 'Five' was a misnomer; there were numbers one to four. She rang the bell marked 'Robin Allgood', grinned and bore it and forced her feet not to take flight and run as fast as they could back to the bus stop, which was what they seriously threatened to do.

He answered the door.

The hallway was morose but not shabby at all: the outside of the house had suggested that it might be. The predominant colour was bottle green, with a lot of gloomy polished mahogany panels on the walls from which brass trays sadly hung. Robin smiled and said hello very quietly, even for him, and then more or less tiptoed upstairs. The reason for all the silence was, he explained later, that his landlady, an old landlady who was allergic to noise and girls, lived in the bottom half of the house and rented the top two floors. To two respectable bachelors, Nuala later learned herself, who took the greatest pains never to disturb her in the slightest way because the rent was low, considering the site of the house and the size of the flats.

Robin's suite consisted of three rooms: considerately he showed all of them to Nuala as soon as they entered. There was an old-fashioned utilitarian kitchen; the table was covered in oilcloth, off-white with a pattern of small red roses on trellis, and extremely worn. The bedroom door he opened hurriedly and then closed again; she caught a glimpse of a largish bed and an outsize walnut wardrobe, dominating the room. The living room was big and had a view of the sea. The furniture was nonedescript—it belonged to the landlady—but it was mainly hidden from view by Robin's books, which were stacked on small free-standing sets of shelves, the kind you can buy for ten pounds at cheap furniture shops, placed all around the walls and across the middle of the floor, where they formed a low wall. 'Can't shelve the walls here, I'm afraid!' shrugged Robin apologetically, because the effect was unusual. 'Landlady wouldn't approve!'

When the tour was over, they sat down on the sofa. This was the only item of furniture in the flat that belonged to him, apart from the bookshelves, and was quite luxurious and modern, a huge deep long sofa covered in cream linen. Unconsciously, Nuala stretched her legs and yawned as soon as she sat down on it: it was conducive to relaxation, that sofa, and she was quite tired by now. Robin, sitting beside her, smiled in a way he had never smiled at her before, and said, 'Nuala, Nuala,' in a voice which was not sad or serious, but a mixture of kind and ironical. He was laughing at someone: her or himself, or perhaps both of them. Helplessly, as if this was his fate and something over which he had no control—or so it seemed—he opened his arms and enclosed her.

She lay against his tweed coat. It smelt of wool, oil, tobacco and middle-aged male sweat. Comforting smells. He did not kiss her or stroke her hair or squeeze her too tightly. Just held her. She felt safe, for the first time in ages. Maybe for the first time ever.

After a while he released her. He was crying slightly, but they sat holding hands and began to chatter a bit aimlessly about how she had travelled out here and what a nice day it was and a lovely dress. Robin got up and went to a dresser in the corner of the room. She thought, happily, that he was going to get something to drink but to her surprise he took from a drawer a brown book. This turned out to be a diary he had been keeping for the past six weeks. It was a blow by blow account of his relationship with her during that period, a sort of *Petit Journal d'Un Grand Passion*. The details were rather ordinary and occasionally unpleasant: 'She is wearing that ugly shirt today.' But it was fulsome in its praise of her charm and personality, and rich in literary allusion.

References to Marta Tikkanen, the author of *Men Cannot Be Raped* naturally abounded, but Shakespeare, WB Yeats, Ronsard and even, once, Patrick Kavanagh, peppered its pages. In short it was an entertaining, clever and flattering document. Nuala enjoyed reading it. She had never read twenty pages devoted more or less exclusively to her before, and realised that she probably never would again.

'Do you always keep a diary?' she asked.

'Oh no, only for special occasions and events, such as this one, ' he said. 'I suppose I needed to express this in writing, for some reason. And I showed it to Fred—you know Fred Maguire, my friend—and asked him for advice?'

'You showed it to Fred?' Nuala felt her heart sink. 'What did he say?'

'He said, "More power to your elbow," which was more or less what I would have expected him to say.'

'Hmm.'

After her reading and some brief discussion of the contents of the diary, they kissed. His face was prickly, like the jacket, and kissing him was different from kissing Erik. But although it was scratchy—maybe he hadn't shaved yet—it felt, again, safe. She did not worry about what he was thinking all the time. She was already beginning to feel that he was a less complex and kinder man than anyone she had been involved with before. That he would never spring some horrible surprise on her or plot, however secretly, against her in his heart. He seemed as straightforward as his tweed jacket.

They ate prawns, in an elegant restaurant with pink table cloths, and drank a nice ice-cold Chablis. She ordered exactly what he chose, mainly because she had a menu without prices which made her suspicious about the cost of the dishes. Over the dessert she hesitated between Gâteau Saint Honore, which she had never had before, and Strawberry Pavlova. But when he decided on plain strawberries and cream she took them too, just to be on the safe side. Besides she needed to lose some weight. She'd put on half a stone since moving to the flat. Half or more. Now she weighed almost nine stones and it just would not do. She could not bear to stand on the scales and see the little hand swinging upwards.

'Without cream,' she said to the waiter, thinking of this.

He talked, as promised, about Finland. But in reality he had little to say about that subject, since he'd only spent a couple of months in Turku and hadn't liked it. He talked about his mother. She talked about her mother. He talked about her trip to Finland, which he did not ask her to cancel. She talked about her trip to Finland. And then, after the strawberries and coffee, when they were having a post-prandial drink in the bar part of the restaurant, he asked her to marry him.

'Gosh,' she said. 'You mean I don't have to go to the pictures with you every Saturday for three years first?'

'I beg your pardon?' he said.

'Well, I mean, gosh, you know…'

'Of course it is a bit precipitate,' he said with a laugh. 'But why waste time? I love you; you seem to like me; I would like to marry you. We don't have to do it straight away, of course, if you'd rather not. Or at all, of course, if you'd rather not.'

'Well,' said Nuala. ' I mean of course it is most awfully nice of you to ask. And I … you know. Gosh.'

'That's marvellous,' said Robin. 'Think it over. You must certainly go to Finland first anyway. I'll come and see you there and you can make up your mind whenever you like.'

'Gosh,' Nuala said, stunned. 'Gosh.'

So this was what being proposed to felt like. Embarrassing.

They slept together that night, having walked home along the seafront in the June twilight. Again a bit precipitate, perhaps, but it seemed to be expected. And again Nuala felt relieved at not having to go to the pictures for a year before that happened.

The only other man she'd slept with had been Erik. Being with Robin was a completely different experience. It was much less intense and acrobatic. It was very much more fun. She didn't think Robin needed to make love to her as urgently as Erik had, which was mildly disconcerting. She was not getting any closer to DH Lawrence type experiences. But she was having a nice time, and Robin did seem interested in practically every part of her body, not just one part. Besides, he kept making little jokes and telling her how beautiful she was, both of which practices she found very civilised. She wondered if he were different from Erik because he was of a different nationality or a different age. Or were all men different? Nobody ever compared notes on things like this, but it would be interesting—comparative sex studies.

She fell asleep, lazily pondering these abtruse but not tormenting problems.

It was late evening on Sunday when she reached home; the morning had been spent lolling about in bed, the afternoon going for a walk by the sea. Robin and she had immediately, now that the status of their relationship was confirmed, established an intimacy. Or perhaps it is truer to say that Nuala no longer felt inhibited in his presence, no longer weighed words and silences. In fact she was often silent with him but now she didn't care. She didn't have to worry about his feelings towards her since she knew what they were worth, more or less, already. His life. He had offered her his life, in exchange, of course, for her own. Still, it was more than a fair bargain in her opinion and she appreciated the gesture very much. Indeed it caused her to glow with a great comfortable sense of her own value. He loved her. And he did not think it was wrong to look for a commitment, that this desire was aberrant in some way.

As she stood on the top of the flight of steps leading from the garden to the hall-door, as she put her key in the lock, Erik appeared behind her.

'Hi!' he said, glumly.

His face was very white. There were deep shadows under his eyes. He looked like a ghost, and, in his incongruous clothing—winter coat, very grubby, jeans and boots—subtly threatening. Nuala felt not just uneasy and guilty, but frightened. Nevertheless she invited him in. ATP.

He deposited himself heavily on her bed, dragged her down beside him and kissed her. His face was prickly too; he hadn't shaven in days. The prickles were softer than Robin's but, in the circumstances, much more vicious. She felt her body growing hard and hostile in his grasp—because that is what it was. She pulled herself away and sat up.

'Mmm!' she said brightly. 'Do you know what: I'm dying for a cup of tea. How about you?'

He stared at her. His blue eyes were still blue. Even the whites were blue, as in those willow-pattern plates where the trees and bridges seem to leak into the white part. The blue-whites were shot with little bloody veins, however, and the pupils were piercing and a bit crazy.

'So where were you?'

'Oh? Out for a walk. I was over seeing my mother.'

'Last night too?'

'Well, yes.'

She did not ask, how did you know I wasn't here last night, but he told her anyway.

'I called at seven and you weren't in. So I stood there, across the road, all night. I know you never came home.'

So that explained the cavernous looks.

Nuala felt weary, all of a sudden, and bored. Exactly the way she'd felt when he'd broken it off with her. Moments of huge significance, moments when life and death decisions could be made. Moments full of potential for tragedy or happiness. And she had to shut herself off. Such moments were too mighty and too abstract; she could not take them.

'How could you?' she said impatiently. If he expected sympathy he had another think coming. 'How could you be so stupid! You'll make yourself ill, behaving like such a fool.'

'I know you weren't at your parents' house. I telephoned.'

'Oh. Well, so what?'

'Where were you?'

'Out. Out. Out.'

She wished he'd leave. She wished more than anything in the world that he'd leave. But she knew he'd go on, inexorably, dragging the truth, which he knew anyway, out of her, torturing her. He'd never really done this before but she knew him, and his ways; she knew that that's what he'd do. And he did. In the end he did not leave. He went to bed, they went to bed together. It was the only way to get him to stop, to shut him up, so she had to do it. And besides she enjoyed comforting him, being maternal. He was such a little boy; he was such a poor vulnerable pathetic creature. She'd always known that, from the very start. She was Nuala again, his own nursemaid, his mummy substitute.

How nice it felt. How natural. How real.

While Robin was in England, Erik came around to the flat almost every day, but not every day, because Vogue had finished her Leaving now and had rung him up. He met her for coffees and drinks occasionally, and told her about his problems with Nuala. He had her deepest sympathy, she said, laughing and tweaking his nose. 'You're an old eejit,' she giggled, 'but I like old eejits!'

Erik did not conceal his relationshop with Vogue from Nuala, and she was comforted by it.

'What do you talk about?' she asked him curiously. Vogue: all she could remember was a rather precious and precocious schoolgirl.

'This and that. She's easy to talk to. Her past.'

Her past?

'Her relationship with her parents and with, you know, boys. How she lost her virginity.'

'Oh! How?'

But he wouldn't tell. The most interesting details were expurgated from his accounts.

Robin sent Nuala a postcard from England. It did not say 'I love you', which she found disappointing, but it signed off 'Love Robin' and she concentrated on that aspect of it. She put it under her pillow and took it out from time to time and rubbed it against her cheek. When Erik was there, she hid it in her handbag.

She did not tell Erik she was planning to marry Robin. It seemed wiser to keep that bit of information to herself for the moment. She was not sure whether the marriage would materialise. Maybe she would change her mind. Maybe Robin would change. People did, about such things. Erik had, for instance. There was no point in showing all your cards to every Tom Dick and Harry. Or to Erik. And Robin had not said, 'I love you' on that postcard. And he had written only once.

Was Erik showing all his to her? She had her doubts, especially on the evenings he did not turn up at her place but spent instead with Vogue.

CHAPTER EIGHTEEN

Two letter-free weeks passed before Robin came back to Dublin. Nuala awaited his return with a mixture of trepidation and hope: she was now completely confused, a befuddled bluebottle at the centre of a spider's web of deception. This was the word she used when she could bear to consider her situation, although she knew it was too grandiose and too outmoded to describe accurately her actions. 'Deception': the word belonged to the same category as 'adultery' or 'sin' or 'hellfire and brimstone'. Its place in the seventies psyche was insecure, to say the least. Free love, sleeping around, grooving: the concept of deceit simply didn't fit in with the ideas of the time. By using it at all she was just turning a mountain into a molehill. Besides, it wasn't as if she were married to anyone. To either of them. She was only attached to both. Attached. Not engaged. Although maybe they both assumed that she was. They both seemed to share a tendency to take this for granted. Indeed, an ability to take for granted that anything important they desired was already achieved was a trait they definitely shared. My wish is everybody's command—that was the belief that seemed to keep them going. A class characteristic, maybe? Well, it was not easy to classify either Robin or Erik socially. Maybe their enviable belief in their own power over destiny was more a mark of masculinity. And of their special cerebral kind of masculinity in particular. Mind over matter and all that. Their minds over her matter.

Nuala's problem was that she was not a real swinger. She was poised on the cusp between the serious past, full of guilt and morals and punishments and restrictions, and the long slide of the post-Beatles, pre-AIDs society. The idea of monogamy was so ingrained in her that she could not cope with seeing two men at the same time, although that might have been the obvious thing to do under the circumstances. Men had done it to her, taking their time while they chose one girl or the other, not telling either what was going on. Erik was doing it right now and that seemed reasonable to everyone, including Nuala. But she couldn't deal with anything as complicated as 'two-timing'. That's the sort of mean thing men are supposed to do. Nice girls like Nuala just couldn't. The fairytale resolution she was seeking would not accommodate that sort of thing at all.

She decided to come straight with Robin as

soon as she met him. It would, in any case, be a way of letting things take 'their natural course'. It would place the ball in her court and free her from the need to make a decision.

He had not asked her to meet him at the airport. She would have liked to, especially as she was going to leave her job anyway and didn't have to hoard her 'leave' anymore. But she had begun to gather that men who travelled regularly did not wish to be met at their points of entry to the country where she was. By her, anyway. She knew when his plane was due; she was to wait for his call.

A sense of *déjà vu* was inevitable, since this is precisely what she had had to do when Erik came home after spending Christmas in Denmark. Sitting in the office, waiting for his ring, she recalled the lines: 'Men may come and men may go/But I go on forever.' I stay on forever seemed to be closer to it.

The thought was depressing. She resolved once again, very firmly, to go to Finland. No matter what they promised or asked or begged or did. I will come and I will go. Going is so important; those who go are those who stay where it counts. In themselves. They are themselves, they have to be, coming and going, going and coming. The ones who wait are something else, bits of someone else. Your life could be spent waiting by a window, twisting your fingers. Images of waiting women came to her: waiting for sailors to come home, waiting for soldiers. Waiting for a cashmere dress from Rouen, waiting for your merchant husband to come back after his three-year voyage to England. Waiting for babies, waiting for children to come from school, husbands to come from work, from conferences, from lecture tours in America. Waiting for life to happen. She wanted to be the one who was waited for, if there had to be such a one.

To her surprise she didn't have long to wait. Robin wasn't the kind of man she was used to; he wasn't the kind of man who kept anyone waiting. She'd hardly started to anticipate his call when he rang, an hour earlier than he had indicated: he'd caught an earlier plane than planned. Would she take a half-day and come out to see him? His voice sounded warm and loving. Listening to it, even for a few minutes, her tension relaxed. Once again she felt that with him she might be able to have a relationship which did not keep her on edge all the time. He would ring when he said he would ring, or earlier. He would not play tricks on her.

They clung to one another—once they had reached the safety of his living room—and were overcome with emotion. He stroked her hair and called her 'my little love'. This was worrying. She was not little. He said, 'I missed you. I really missed you, my little darling,' and it sounded as if he meant it. Even more worrying. But nice.

He had on a new shaving lotion, which made him smell more glamorous than before. For her, he said. And to her he gave a tiny bottle of Chanel Number 5. He put some on his thick, smoky finger and dabbed it behind her ears. He took her hand and pushed it through his hair, which was washed, shiny, cleaner looking than before.

It had seemed like a year, he said. His mother had irritated the life out of him. He never wanted to leave her—that is, Nuala—again.

She didn't tell him then. How could she? He needed her. His love was true.

She told Erik instead. The next evening, when he came around. What she told him was that she and Robin were going to get married.

'I love you too,' he said, angrily. 'I need you too.'

He was also looking very well: he had new blue jeans and a light-blue shirt with thin yellow stripes, and he was shaving properly again and washing. His fair hair had grown long and fluffed over his forehead, softening his face. He looked young and vulnerable. He looked like a baby, by comparison with Robin.

'Yes,' she said. 'Well.'

If you hadn't messed around none of it

would have happened. And I wouldn't be forced to make this impossible decision.

'Look, Nuala. We've been together for a long time. We've had a lot of experiences together. We're good for each other, we really are. You know it. We belong together.'

This was not empty rhetoric. He believed it.

Nuala believed it, up to a point, too. She put her arms around him and closed her eyes. She could not make this decision. She simply could not.

Vogue laughed and laughed when Erik told her about it all, the next day. 'Serves you right!' she said. 'You're an awful messer. But I like messers!'

Clever Vogue.

She helped Erik clean up his flat. She had time on her hands now that the Leaving was over. She would be going to Brittany with her family in August, on a camping holiday, but for now she was resting after the examinations. She found the letters from his mother.

'You mean you haven't even looked at them? Jesus, I knew you were thick but I didn't think you were a complete imbecile. There could be something wrong with her. Anything could have happened. Read them.'

He read them.

His mother had left Elsa. Or Elsa had left his mother, or something. She, his mother, was no longer sure that she was a lesbian; it looked as if it might have been a mistake. She was in therapy and doing very well. She hoped this news did not shock him; she was sorry to have caused him such upset. But she'd had to experiment, she'd had to explore her feelings. Anyone could make a mistake.

This was all in an April letter. Just before the letters had stopped.

'Phone her.'

He phoned. There was no reply.

She was in hospital. She was ill. She was dying of some unmentionable disease, or of heartache, betrayed by husband, son, lover. Betrayed by all she had ever cared for.

'Don't be so dramatic. Try her again tomorrow night.'

She answered herself. Sorry, she'd been at a movie in town. *Alice Doesn't Live Here Anymore!* Have you seen it yet? It is wonderful, just wonderful. She was perfectly all right, still in Charlottenlund, alone, it seemed, in the house. Was he coming home soon? Yes, he said, he was. For a while, at least.

'You can leave your things at my place,' said Vogue. 'I'll bring the car around to collect them.'

'Oh good!' said Nuala. 'I'm so glad. I never thought they belonged together, really. I didn't like Elsa, for some reason, did you? She seemed so hard.'

She was glad to hear that he was going home, too. She liked to think of him safe in Copenhagen while she was in Finland. Safe with Mother. Away from Vogue.

'You can leave your things at my parents' house,' she offered kindly. 'If you're not taking them all with you.'

'Its OK. Vogue's taking them.'

Nuala felt her stomach contract, in its familiar old position, for a second.

'She's got a car, it's easier.'

'Her own car?'

'Well, it's her mother's, I believe. She uses it from time to time.'

Once Mollie had decided she wanted to learn to drive. Dessie, who had driven all his life and drove skilfully but badly, took her out for a lesson. On the first lesson, she crashed into the wall of the car-park they were practising in and smashed the bonnet of the car, an eight-year old Volkswagen. She had refused to take further lessons. Dessie chauffeured her everywhere. None of his children had ever dreamed of trying to drive his car, although Christopher actually could drive now and had his own banger. It was a class-distinguisher, the car. The distinction was not so much between those who possessed them and those who didn't, as between those who drove them and those who didn't. Working class women didn't,

ELIZABETH O'HARA

working class girls didn't, even though their husbands or fathers might own some sort of car, held together with wires and hope. Middle-class women had, at this stage, their own Minis or Fiats and they lent them to their daughters all the time. No doubt it was one of those things that cemented the mother-daughter relationship, or fouled it up completely. Mollie had had nothing, apart from her affection, to give to her daughters. Not even driving lessons. Not even advice that made any sense in their world. Nuala imagined Vogue, chirpy and cheeky, with her mother. Smart, cool, languid. Beautiful, because men like Vogue's father, successful men with lots of money, married only beautiful wives. Everyone knew what their motivation was. Poor men could afford to marry for character and sweetness of expression, things like that. And so academics could, if they were not perfectionists about female beauty, which most of them were. Although not, apparently, Robin.

Nuala went to visit Mary towards the end of July, shortly before she was due to leave for Finland. She had not seen her, or heard from her, in ages. Even Mollie had not seen her. Mary phoned from time to time promising to call around, but she never did. Mollie, used to eccentric behaviour from her daughters, was growing more and more anxious. But she did nothing about it because she didn't know what to do.

Mary was sitting in the back yard when she arrived, on a plastic garden chair with a horrible pattern of brown flowers on it and a rusty tray on spindly legs at her feet. She unfolded a second plastic chair, one with red and white stripes, for Nuala and they both sat down in the sunshine.

Mary's appearance had altered drastically since Nuala had last met her, eight weeks before. In that same period, great changes had occurred in her own life but she believed that she still looked much the same as she had at any time over the past few years. Mary, on the other hand, had literally gone to seed. So had her little garden. Both wore the same sad and frowsy air; both were overblown and wasted. Mary, dressed in an uncharacteristically unflattering blue smock with a red bow at the neck, was fatly pregnant. Her complexion was blotchy, red rather than sallow. Her hair, which looked as if it hadn't been washed in weeks, trailed in greasy tails around her shoulders. She was a wreck.

The garden—and the house, but it had always been a bit like that—was in a similar state. The once bouyant parsley patch was now inhabited by a few burnt brown stalks of the same herb and a profusion of dandelion clocks. Otherwise the only plants in the garden were some very high wild buddleia growing out of cracks in the walls and copious strings of Robin-in-the-hedge choking the herbaceous border. On the concrete yard which constituted the greater part of the garden were two coffee cups, a plastic bag and an empty tomato purée can. By the outer wall was a pile of empty wine bottles.

'So you're off on Saturday?' Mary asked, in a lazy voice.

'Yes, I am.'

'Aren't you lucky?' Deep sigh. Wan smile.

'I suppose so. There are other way of being lucky.'

'Mmm.' She seemed too exhausted to bother being sceptical. She looked as Nuala had hoped neither of them ever would look: resigned to the awfulness of life. A martyr to reality.

'Would you like something to drink? Some of John's wine?'

'That would be nice.' Nuala was thirsty. It was a bit hot for wine—wine and sun don't go together. But the atmosphere needed something to dilute its tension. 'That's a good idea.'

Mary got up and moved heavily and unsteadily across the concrete. She wore no stockings, and had flip-flops instead of shoes. That could have accounted for the slight unsteadiness of her gait. But as Nuala observed the rusty tray, her red face, the grubby garden, the truth began to dawn on her.

Mary returned in a few minutes, with an uncorked bottle and two lemonade glasses which were not particularly clean. She put the glasses on the tray and filled them to the brim.

'That's a lot, isn't it?' said Nuala. 'Aren't you supposed to be off this kind of thing for the moment?'

'Of course I am,' she said crossly. 'I'm supposed to be off drink, cigarettes, coffee, decent food, work...I'm off the lot, supposed to be.'

'Oh dear.' Nuala was at a loss. She drank some wine. It had a ripe musty taste which she did not relish. A moment elapsed in silence. Mary drank about half her glass.

'Aren't you happy?' Nuala grasped wildly for something to say.

'Of course I'm happy,' she said. It didn't sound ironic or false, but if it were true, life was more complicated than Nuala had imagined. She had never seen Mary look more miserable.

'Good,' she said, hoping for elaboration. But none came. Mary was back in her shell again. All she did was lob back the question. And Nuala, who wanted to discuss Erik and Robin with someone, some human being, before she went off to where they'd constitute an unreal subject that would bore everybody's pants off, presuming she ever did get to know anybody there in the first place, said that she was. She resigned herself, like Mary. She would not be discussing Erik and Robin. Ever. With anyone. They were her problem, of interest to no one but herself.

'You're doing the right thing,' Mary said with some vehemence. 'No matter how you feel, you must go to Finland. And actually you should probably stay there.'

'Always, you mean?'

'Nobody ever says always. It's in bad taste, that word. But there's nothing here for people like us. There just isn't anything. If you stay, or if you come back, your life will be dull, it will be ruined. You won't have a career, you won't have fulfilment, you won't even have money or glamour, not that that matters much. But you'll get nowhere, absolutely nowhere. It is hopeless in this country. It's important to realise that in time.'

'Are you sure?'

'Of course I'm sure. Look at you. Look at me.'

Nuala looked. Mary's face had turned red, with wine or anger.

'I don't think I care about all those things you mentioned, actually. I'm sure there are more important things, like love and families and so on.'

'Families! What does our family mean to us? I mean, that's a pleasant pious sentiment, but don't talk to me about families. I mean to say I haven't seen Mum and Dad in seven months.

They don't seem to care. I don't either, and that's the point. All that sort of thing is unimportant. What is important is the way life is lived. At half-pressure. I feel I'm only half-alive all the time—you know what I mean?'

'Yes.'

She meant she was drunk, in more ways than one. She meant that as far as she was concerned you had to be drunk (in more ways than one) in order to survive at all, in Ireland.

'Don't you want it? The baby, I mean?'

'Don't I want it? I want it more than I've ever wanted anything. Believe it or not. But I know what it means as far as my life is concerned. I know that too.'

'You mean…it inhibits you…'

'Yes, I bloody well mean that. It is likely to cramp my style a bit, don't you think? Can't you imagine for a minute what it will all mean?'

'I think it would be nice. I'd like a baby myself.'

'I'd like one too. Oh yes, I would. But not yet, Lord.'

'It will grow, Mary. And there are crèches and things anyway. You don't have to be stuck with it all the time.'

'Oh yes, you do. That's the one thing you do have to be. You get it and it's yours for ever after. You'll realise that if it ever happens to you.'

Three days later, Nuala left the country.

Erik had returned to Copenhagen the day before so she had already said farewell to him. He was going to write, he was going to come and visit her at Christmas. Robin and she had had a goodbye dinner in the restaurant at Dalkey. Afterwards they walked along by the sea in the balmy summer air and watched the lights twinkling on Howth Head. Robin had sung 'The Carnival is Over', which was a little depressing. It has an air of finality, that song, and Nuala found it is hard to give up anything, no matter what, no matter how beneficial the sacrifice was likely to be. But afterwards he softened the blow, as people do. He would write. He would come over to visit her at Christmas. The long-term future was not mentioned by either of them: it is such a delicate issue, and difficult to discuss in a collected manner.

She decided to wait and see which of them would come to see her. To see if either of them would. She did not know. She thought it would be Robin: so far word and action had always been the same with him. But she did not know. Christmas and Finland seemed centuries away, to her. Anything could happen between now and then, between Ireland and there. They would all bide their time; they would wait and see. Time could shoulder the responsibility and that was just fine as far as Nuala was concerned. All her life so far she had been accepting other people's decisions—her teachers', her parents'. The decisions of interview boards, the decisions of society. In the area of relationships she had usually chosen the kind of men who kept her at the begging end, the kind of men who made all the decisions themselves. Now when she had two such men, complicated, powerful men, begging her for something—for her love, or for herself?—she did not know how to choose. The only thing to do was to continue to lead her own life and to get away from both of them. To move on and see what would happen next.

What she did not realise then was that that was a decision in itself.

Nuala said goodbye to her mother at Exeter Place (where she had stayed on the last night, having moved out of the flat). She preferred to go alone to the airport, but she felt very lonely waving goodbye to Mollie, who looked forlorn and vulnerable, as she stood by the rusty iron gate. The sense of loneliness, the sense of being hollow, continued as the taxi drove down Rathmines Road and over Portobello Bridge, past Camden Street and Avondale Terrace where Mary was sitting in her garden— boozing, probably—past the stalls where Nuala had been buying vegetables and fruit on water-coloured spring Saturdays a few months ago,

before Finland and Robin and the return of
Erik. There had been a gloomy aspect to all of
that at the time. But already she could hardly
recall suffering, and a rosy glow was settling
over her memory of the months in the flat, of
working in the Civil Service, of being an
independent single girl. She had come very
close to happiness there at some point just
before she leaped back on the merry-go-round.
It would have been nice if it had all lasted just a
little longer. But the one thing she did know
now was that you can't make things last longer
than they are destined to last. The only thing to
do when you are twenty-two is to set out on the
adventures that are offered to you even though
you have no idea where they may lead.

As she passed O'Connell Bridge and the
busy parts of the city her sadness lifted. And as
they drove along the wide straight Swords
Road which leads to the airport and which,
because of the flatness of the district
surrounding, seems to lead to the sky, she
began to feel exhilarated. Already she felt she
was in the air. Already she was soaring over the
rooftops of Dublin, over Howth and Ireland's
Eye and the Irish Sea. Over Wales and the
North Sea, over Erik, in Copenhagen, over the
Baltic to the beginning of the eastern world.

And it felt good to be setting off. It felt like
the air on her skin on one of those days in mid-
March when there is some warmth in the sun

for the very first time, and the daffodils are blooming in sheltered places and the leaves on the early shrubs, the redcurrants, are out, and there is a faint background twitter of birds, and for the first time since September you can sit in the garden and have lunch there. It felt like that.

It felt right.

More books from
Attic & Basement Press

Whispers in the Wind
by Mary Ryan

A magnificent saga of love and intrigue set in Ireland
during the turbulent years of the 1920s.

£4.99

Glenallen
by Mary Ryan

Three young women become friends at boarding school in
Ireland during the 1930s and soon they become intwined
under the influence of Glenallen.

£4.99

Promised
by Joan O'Neill

A tale of forbidden passion between a nun and a priest.

£4.99

The Quest
by Heather Von Prondynski

At thirty Maggie decides that she wants both a child
and her career as lecturer at Trinity, but not necessarily
a marriage. A love story with adventurous mishaps.

£5.99

---

*IF YOU WISH YOU CAN ORDER YOUR COPIES
DIRECT FROM US BY PHONE, FAX OR POST.*

Attic Press,
4 Upper mount Street, Dublin 2. Ireland.
Tel: (01) 661 6128 Fax: (01) 661 6176